Praise for Dr. Cory Cohen Mysteries

"A genuine page-turner in the best sense. Her years as a psychologist have earned Ceren a look at the darkness of the psyche and human behavior. Psychologist-sleuth—Cory Cohen—is both compassionate and tough. A strong, heartfelt work from a writer we will be hearing a lot."

T. Jefferson Parker, *Edgar-winning author*

"This is a good fun thriller that packs in a whole lot of themes, in a way that doesn't clash. While being entertained, the reader is likely to get some subtle education on a number of psychological matters such as eating disorders and the effects of trauma."

Bob Rich, PhD, author *Anikó: The Stranger Who Loved Me*

"Riveting, tightly woven mystery screeches to a satisfying conclusion bringing together all the pieces of this intiguiging puzzle. A terrific whodunit spun around the dynamics of psychotherapy. This would make a terrific film."

Maryanne Raphael, Editor, *Writers World*

"Of interest not only to psychologists and patients, but to mystery fans. It has all the elements of suspense and drama : a clever plot and interesting well drawn characters."

Andrew Duggan, M.D.

"Author Sandra Ceren draws upon her thirty years of clinical work with crime victims to bring a degree of realism and accuracy that is rarely matched and never surpassed."

Midwest Book Review

"Another exciting, engrossing psychological thriller from a favorite author. The well-defined characters and intrigue create a compelling page-turner to the very end."

Holly A. Hunt, Ph.D. psychologist, author, speaker

Vanished

A Dr. Cory Cohen Psychological Thriller

Sandra Levy Ceren

Modern History Press

VANISHED: A Dr. Cory Cohen Psychological Thriller
Copyright © 2014 by Sandra Levy Ceren
from the Dr. Cory Cohen Mysteries Series

Library of Congress Cataloging-in-Publication Data

Ceren, Sandra Levy.
  Vanished : a Dr. Cory Cohen psychological thriller / by Sandra
Levy Ceren.
      pages cm
  ISBN 978-1-61599-230-0 (pbk. : alk. paper) -- ISBN 978-1-
61599-231-7 (ebook)
  1. Women psychotherapists--Fiction. 2. Private investigators--
Fiction. 3. Missing persons--Fiction. 4. San Diego (Calif.)--Fiction.
I. Title.
  PS3603.E697V36 2014
  813'.6--dc23
                                                    2014006546

Distributed by Ingram Book Group (USA/CAN), Bertram's Books
(UK), Hachette Livre (FR)

Modern History Press, an imprint of
Loving Healing Press
5145 Pontiac Trail
Ann Arbor, MI 48105
Tollfree 888-761-6268
FAX 734-663-6861

info@ModernHistoryPress.com
www.ModernHistoryPress.com

The Dr. Cory Cohen Mysteries

- *Prescription for Terror*
- *Stolen Secrets*
- *Imposter for Hire*
- *Vanished*

Learn more about Dr. Sandra L. Ceren, read blog postings, and the latest news at www.SandraLevyCerenPhd.com.

Prologue

With her body and personal belongings stored in the trunk of his leased Lincoln Town Car, he slowly motored up the coast marked "Highway 101." As far as he could see, his was the only vehicle on the road. The radio announcer rattled on about "hazardous conditions and pea-soup fog." He couldn't comprehend what that meant, but figured it had to do with poor visibility. He assured himself that the fog was a good thing. It would shield him from being seen when he dumped the body. He was confident in the GPS to safely navigate him to the beach.

Suddenly, he heard a moan. It seemed to come from the rear of the car. It made him shudder. Suppose she wasn't dead? He imagined her stirring, still alive. "She's harmless, and if she's not dead now, she will be by the time I'm finished with her," he muttered.

A moment later, he detected another soft moan. Was there a problem with the car? "*Merde!*" he shouted. He had leased the Lincoln because of its reputation for reliability, quiet, and oversized trunk.

He listened for more noise, but it had stopped. Heaving a deep sigh, he told himself it must have been his imagination.

He reviewed what had happened earlier. Killing her had not been in his plan, but rage had overtaken him. He hated her for his dependence on the proceeds from her remarkable work, but now that was over.

His only mistake was that he should have killed her insufferable spoiled brat too. She could make serious trouble for him. If she had been home instead of taking care of a sick neighbor, the angel-brat would be dead now, too.

He must return to the house and kill her tonight. He'd make it look like she had walked in on a robbery and was killed by the robber.

With the brat gone, as her mother's partner and manager, he alone would possess her valuable sculpture and antique collection.

Grinning, he congratulated himself on his good fortune that the work of prominent dead artists commanded a higher price.

Suddenly, he became painfully aware of his full bladder. He was desperate to urinate, but he couldn't make out a safe place to stop. Fear crept up on him, like a vicious beast. The GPS instructed him to make a left turn at the next street for the beach. He would head to a place to park, pee, and drag the body onto the beach under the cover of dense fog.

He stopped at the red signal light and peered around. He could barely make out what appeared to be rocks on the side of the highway. Could this be a picnic site? A parking area? Was this on the shore? As instructed by the GPS, he made a left turn. He parked at the side of the road. Pressing the trunk button to *open*, he stepped out of the car.

Blinded by fog, he tripped on a huge boulder and fell on a rock. He tried to stand, but the pain in his ankle was excruciating. Forcing himself to endure, he dragged his foot, twisted and turned his body toward the car trunk, and pulled out her body. He wrapped the king-sized blanket around the body and dragged the load toward the sound of crashing waves. On the way, he wet his pants. Cursing under his breath, he tripped and fell several times before the surf splashed his ankles.

Determined to make her death look like a drowning accident, he lifted the body and carried it into the ocean.

Waist-deep, he held onto the body, planning to release it further in before swimming back to shore. Suddenly, the undertow knocked him off his feet. In the fog, he couldn't see how far he was from shore. Trapped into the rip current, he was pulled further off shore into deeper water. He tried to fight off the terror, but things happened too fast. Desperately, he held on to her body as a life raft, until a powerful rip separated him from it, sucking him in, deeper and deeper.

⚡ 1 ⚡

Cory couldn't shake an odd feeling—like a hint of doom lurking on the horizon as she peered out her office window, at another glorious day in southern California. Hummingbirds hovered over the red and yellow rose bushes in search of choice nectar and a gentle breeze brushed the quivering leaves on the palm tree. Despite the tranquil scene, she stiffened in expectation.

The doorbell rang, jolting her in surprise as no one was expected until a few hours later. She checked the security video screen. Recognizing her postman, she opened the door. He handed her a certified letter requiring her signature. Although the sender's name was unfamiliar, she signed for the letter.

Seated at her uncluttered teak desk, she tore open the sealed envelope, and gasped as she read:

> Doctor Cohen,
>
> This is to alert you that your bad advice has caused me grave consequences for which you are professionally responsible.
>
> My attorney states you have committed malpractice. He recommends I request a five thousand dollar certified bank check from you made out to CAROLE ROY and sent to P.O.B. 666, Oceanside, CA.
>
> You have one week to stop the case from going forward. I assure you, if you don't comply with this request, you will regret it.
>
> The cost of my litigation will be your responsibility. Your income, your reputation, and your license are at stake.
>
> > Your former patient,
> > Carole Roy

Startled, and almost overcome by a queasy feeling, her hands trembled as she placed the letter on her desk.

The sender's name was totally unfamiliar to her. After reading the letter again, she figured it must be a hoax—mischief from a sociopath, a blackmailer, probably sending the same letter to select professionals practicing in wealthy areas across the country, gambling on the possibility someone would just pay to avoid the hassle.

Cory strongly doubted that any intelligent person would fall for such a scheme.

Although she regarded the letter as a threat without a shred of substance, she knew she had to do something about it as soon as possible.

She thumbed through her file cabinet crammed with the last seven years of patient records as required by the California Psychology Licensing Board. She had carefully stored her files within partitions representing each of the last seven years. Every case that had ended during that time frame was filed alphabetically within the appropriate section. It took her over half an hour to reveal, just as she had figured, that no one by the name Carole Roy had been her patient in the past seven years.

Cory shook her head. Perhaps a person identifying herself as Carole Roy had made an appointment, but had not shown up for it.

She ran her fingers down the pages of her current appointment book dated from the last five months, but the name did not appear.

She whipped out her last two years of appointment books from the file drawer. Finally, she found "Carole Roy" scrawled with a fine line drawn across it next to a phone number. *NS*—the notation she used for "no show"—appeared next to Wednesday 4:00 p.m. exactly two years ago.

Out of curiosity, she called the number. It belonged to a tailor unfamiliar with anyone named Carole Roy.

"Has anyone else called asking for this person?" Cory asked.

"No. I'd remember. We don't get many calls, being new to the neighborhood," the man said.

Cory phoned several local colleagues and a few practicing in wealthy areas across the country. She figured a blackmailer would target practitioners with deep pockets. If her calls weren't fruitful, she would have to fish in a larger pool—an annoying, time-consuming task.

Cory called fifteen psychologists. None were available to speak with her. She left messages requesting a call back on her mobile, hoping to learn if any were afflicted by the same bug and were willing to discuss the situation.

Blackmail was considered a crime, a statutory offense. If she could establish a high volume of complaints of attempted blackmail made to mental health professionals, it could result in quicker action from authorities and prevent future threats.

If she were the only professional known to have received such a threat, she would immediately consult her malpractice insurance attorney.

Re-reading the certified letter, she stopped at the paragraph citing the post office box number 666 and smiled. "666" equals sick, sick, sick," she murmured. Chuckling, she began to feel better.

Cory figured the blackmailer could be a mentally ill person who sought retribution for some negative psychotherapy experience.

More likely, the blackmailer learned about billing and records and malpractice in some other way, and regarded a psychologist as an easy target. Perhaps the blackmailer had worked in the billing department of a health care facility.

Powerless to immediately change the situation, Cory realized she needed to distract herself from worrying about it. She would take the advice she gave to patients: worry is a counterproductive waste of energy.

Glad for the extra set of running gear she stored at the office, she decided to spend the free time relieving her tension by running on the beach. She expected to come back energized by endorphins, and better able to cope with the distressing blackmail letter.

Tucking her long, black hair into a ponytail, she noticed it was the proper length for a donation to the Wigs for Kids project. Her good deed—a traditional *mitzvah* would uplift her spirits. She grabbed the phone and made an appointment.

Wig makers preferred Asian hair. Cory's contributions were reminders of her bi-racial heritage—a Japanese mother she had never known, who preferred an international musical career to a family.

Cory never experienced anger toward the unknown birth mother; rather she felt privileged to be raised by her loving paternal Jewish grandparents.

Just as she was about to change her clothes, she heard a buzz at the front door.

The image of a pale young woman with a distraught expression on her face appeared on the security video screen.

"May I help you?" Cory asked

"I so much hope you can. I'm desperate and need to see you right away. Ann referred me," pleaded the woman.

Responding to what could be an emergency, Cory buzzed her in and hurried to greet her at the front door.

The young woman followed Cory from the cozy reception room into the office.

Petite, with small facial features, brown eyes and dark blonde hair neatly rolled into a bun, she appeared to be in her twenties. Her black suit and white blouse were well tailored and somber, next to her pale face.

She scanned the room, furnished with teak chairs, table, and desk, and ran her hand over the top of the soft black leather couch. She seemed unduly cautious of her surroundings, like an animal sniffing around a new environment to determine if it was safe.

She paused to examine Cory's framed credentials on the wall. Supposedly reassured, she turned to the books lining the shelves as though shopping for the right one that would hold a solution to her vexing problem.

From desperation to uncertainty about her surroundings, she seated herself opposite Cory, leaned forward, and rested her hands on her lap.

Pad and pen on her lap, Cory asked, "What's your name?"

"That's just it. I don't know who I am."

≈ 2 ≈

Cory took a deep breath. "Please explain."

"At eight this morning, an alarm clock awakened me. When I opened my eyes, I was shocked to find myself in an unfamiliar room. I felt so weird—so incredibly strange.

"At first I thought I was dreaming—or sleepwalking. My heart thumped so loudly, I felt the vibration in my ears. I leaped out of bed and feverishly searched the room. I opened the closet and saw several garments. At first I wasn't sure if they were mine, but they seemed to be my size and my style. The shoes fit me, too."

She pulled out a tissue from the nearby box, and dabbed her moist brow. "I'm terrified. I don't know what happened to me." Trembling, she hugged herself and rocked back and forth like a baby wrapped in the safety of her mother's arms.

"I also found several books. The titles were vaguely familiar. I skimmed through a few to see if they stirred my memory, but they didn't. Perhaps they were new and I hadn't read them yet—or I'm really going crazy. This is too, too scary."

"Your experience doesn't mean you've gone crazy, but it certainly is frightening. Did you check other rooms in the house?"

"Yes. At first I was afraid to leave the room, scared of what I'd find. I forced myself to peek out the door. I listened for some sounds of life, like footsteps, voices, running water, but I heard nothing. Although it was quiet, I tiptoed out and looked around. All the rooms were empty. It's as if everyone moved out while I was asleep."

"Who moved out?"

"I don't know." She buried her face in her hands and sobbed.

"I understand this is frustrating, but you will regain your memory. You said Ann referred you. Can you recall anything about that?"

"No, I don't remember anything at all. I found your card in a purse. Ann's name is written on the back." She pulled out a card from her pocket and handed it to Cory.

During many years of practice, Cory had never seen anyone with this kind of amnesia. She had treated people who had forgotten bits and pieces of important memory, but this was different. She knew the causes could be from a head injury, drug or alcohol usage, or a traumatic event.

Fortunately, a highly respected medical group was a few steps away in the next building.

"Did you find anything to identify you in the room?"

The young woman removed an expensive looking leather wallet from her purse and handed it to Cory. It contained a driver's license and a Visa card both bearing the name Ashley P. Hogan.

"Ashley Hogan?" Cory asked.

"I've run that name through my head over and over, but it means nothing to me," the young woman replied.

Cory examined the license bearing a photo of an excellent likeness of the woman in front of her.

"The DMV has a thumb print on file which could prove if you are Ashley Hogan."

"DMV?"

"Yes. The Department of Motor Vehicles."

"Oh, yes, of course. Must I go there to be fingerprinted?"

Cory shook her head. "No. When I needed my fingerprints to renew my psychology license, a local store with a special machine took my fingerprints and filed them with the FBI and the Department of Justice."

Ashley shook her head. "I know in my heart I'm not a criminal and I don't want to go through all that."

"It is a nuisance, but it would reassure you of your identity. An easier way is for a nearby notary agent to take your thumb print, but you'd still need a government agency to identify it."

"Suppose they do verify that I am Ashley P. Hogan—so what? It wouldn't bring back my memory."

"That's true, but it is a starting place." Cory replied.

"I don't know why, but I'm afraid of government authorities."

Cory considered the possibility that Ashley's loss of memory was due to having witnessed something dreadful. Dreadful enough to block a major part of her memory, but still keeping a self-protective sliver.

Cory loved solving mysteries and this one presented a huge challenge.

"In the house did you notice a computer, tablet, or any electronic device such as a cell phone that stores data?" Cory asked. "It may help jog your memory."

"No. The only room furnished was the one that must be mine—judging from the clothes—otherwise the place was totally empty. If I had a phone, I'd have called before coming here." Ashley's voice held a tone of exasperation.

"I understand your frustration. I'll make a copy of your driver license for your chart. Would you allow me to contact a former FBI agent—now a trustworthy private investigator? Perhaps he could find information about you."

Ashley nodded and without hesitation signed her name on the release form.

"Instinctively, you knew how to sign your name," Cory said. "This is a really good sign."

The young woman shrugged. She began to sob, cupping her hands over her face.

Cory handed her a tissue and watched the frustrated young woman dab at her tears.

"But I have no memory of a past. I don't know anything about myself."

"You have an excellent chance to recover your memory. Amnesia—a loss of memory—is treatable."

"What causes it?"

Cory hesitated, unwilling to make the woman more anxious. "Perhaps a bad drug, or too much alcohol."

"I didn't notice any alcohol or pill bottles. I told you the house was empty apart from the room where I had awakened."

Cory considered the possibility that Ashley could have been given an injectable substance like scopolamine. It was unlikely that whoever injected her would leave evidence behind.

It seemed more likely Ashley had witnessed a traumatic event or had sustained a head injury.

"Are you feeling pain anywhere?"

The tearful woman shook her head.

Cory took notes. "Are you experiencing any physical symptoms?"

"My heart is still racing. I feel chilled and a bit weak."

"Probably because you're frightened. I'll refer you to Doctor Green in the next building for a complete physical exam."

Cory trusted Mimi Green's medical acumen. She'd know the best way to proceed would likely include blood work and a urine sample. The neurological exam, functional MRI or a CT scan, would probably occur at one of the many hospitals nearby.

"Do you think I may have a brain tumor?"

"It's doubtful. Let's not consider that at the moment."

"What else can it be?" A pained expression etched deep furrows on her forehead.

Cory hesitated. "Sometimes amnesia occurs after a person witnesses a traumatic event."

Ashley shuddered. "I can't imagine what horror that could be."

"Let's not go there yet. Amnesia may be protective for now."

"No. I've got to remember. I must. I must. This is hell," Ashley cried.

Cory handed her the box of tissues. "I'm confident that your memory will return. If the loss is from a drug or too much alcohol, your amnesia could clear up in hours or a few days."

"What if I witnessed something horrendous?"

"You'll grow stronger. You'll be able to deal with it."

Cory called Mimi Green's private line and reached her immediately. Fortunately, Mimi had the time to provide a thorough exam after Cory completed her session with Ashley.

"We're in luck. Dr. Green can see you after we finish our session."

"I'm very grateful to you for setting this up for me so quickly," Ashley said, trembling. "Frankly, I'm afraid of the exam and the results."

"I can imagine how difficult the situation is for you. I assure you that the exam is not intrusive. It doesn't hurt. You're in competent hands with Doctor Green. I have a light schedule and will help you through this trying time."

"That is comforting. Thank you," Ashley said.

Anticipating that she would gain more insight about this woman from her graphic productions than the amnesic woman could otherwise provide, Cory handed her a clipboard, a sketchpad pad, and a pencil.

"Please draw a house on page one, a person on page two, and a tree on page three."

Ashley took the materials and began to sketch, her furrowed brow softening with each stroke of the pencil. Like an accomplished artist on her own turf, she made bold, confident strokes, lost in an altered state of consciousness. She took more time on the task, much longer than most others confronted with the same assignment. It seemed to help her relax into a familiar activity.

Cory smiled as she witnessed the telling transformation.

When Ashley finished, she calmly handed the drawing materials to Cory.

"An artist finds drawing cathartic," Cory remarked.

"I'm glad you asked me to do that. It felt right. It felt like me… whoever I am… like I'm discovering a part of myself."

"We've made a fine start. We know you're a very good artist—perhaps an accomplished one."

The amateur detective, a role Cory frequently assumed, had surfaced. Detection was the part of psychology she found most intriguing.

"You're a very interesting young woman. When you came into my office, despite your anxiety, you took the time to examine my credentials. It suggests you're a cautious, intelligent person. Ann had given you my card, so you probably met at the university because she spent much of her time there. Perhaps she mentioned she worked for me. Maybe you asked for my card because you or someone close to you had a problem."

"That makes sense." Ashley leaned forward. "But how can I recollect it, when I've lost my memory? Oh, this is so frustrating." She stamped her foot as though it would loosen the lock on her memory bank.

"I'll do my best to help you regain your memory. Do you mind answering a few more questions?"

Ashley shrugged. "I don't know if I can answer them."

"It's about items in your house. Stop me when you've had enough."

Ashley nodded assent.

"Were there textbooks, a calendar, or an appointment book, from the place you just left?" Cory asked.

Ashley closed her eyes for a few seconds. "No."

"Did you check closets, drawers, purses, pockets for these items?"

"Actually, I did. Nothing gave me a clue, except from the two items in my wallet."

"Do you have a mailbox key?"

Ashley checked her key ring. "I have a house key and a car key. The car key has the car manufacturer's logo on it, so I figured it belonged to the car in front of the house. I searched inside the car and trunk for something to trigger a memory, but there wasn't anything except legal papers related to the car."

"Among the papers in your car, were there any business cards, such as an insurance agent's?"

Ashley shook her head. "I wish there were."

"Is there a private mailbox near the house?"

The young woman paused to reflect. "Yes. I think so."

"Good. When you open your mail, something may jog your memory. Another thing that may help would be to call the number on the back of your credit card and request a current statement."

Ashley sobbed softly as tears ran down her cheeks.

Cory pushed the tissue box closer to Ashley. "Your situation is frustrating right now, but I'm confident that it is temporary. "

Ashley nodded. "You mean I can recover—if I survive. You must understand I'm terrified because I suspect someone knew I had lost my memory and is determined to keep me in the dark. That's the reason I couldn't find any memorabilia such as family photos or birth certificates or passports to help me remember."

Cory pondered Ashley's explanation, but chose not to fan the flames of fear. "You can't be sure about that, but it shows your reasoning isn't compromised."

"Thank God for that blessing." Ashley placed her hands in a prayer position and tilted her head upwards.

Was Ashley religious, as her gesture seemed to suggest? If so, would her attendance at a church service trigger memories? Cory considered the possibility. However, Ashley's prayer gesture was a common one that some people use to make a point. If she didn't regain her memory in a reasonable time, a visit to a church could be used to stir remembrances of any number of important past events: a marriage, baptism, confirmation, funeral, or a holiday celebration.

Cory decided to wait until the results of the exam came in before making the suggestion. For now, she would help Ashley sort out her immediate practical needs.

"It may be wise to call a security company to install equipment," Cory suggested.

"Oh, no. I'd feel safer in a hotel."

"Of course, that's a much better choice. It shows your judgment hasn't been compromised." Cory handed her a pad and pencil. "Make some notes about a few things you can do for now."

Ashley looked up at Cory, like a secretary ready for dictation.

"Purchase a monthly cell phone service to protect your privacy. You can open one up at a nearby electronics store. Please call me with your new number."

Ashley gripped the pencil tightly as she made notes.

"Rent a mail box at a convenient post office, and report the new mailing address to the Visa card company. The number is on the back of your card."

"What if my Visa statement doesn't jog my memory? What if the damage is permanent?" Ashley sobbed.

"I doubt that is the case. You'll have a thorough examination by doctors—experts in their fields."

Cory glanced at the clock on the wall. "I think it's nearly time for your appointment with Doctor Green. She'll help figure out the cause of your amnesia. The exam is painless and results are usually available fairly soon. Spend some time drawing—whatever comes to mind." She handed Ashley a sketchpad and a packet of pastels stored in her desk from an old art class. "It may make you feel better."

"Thanks very much. I'll draw something for you," Ashley dropped two one-hundred dollar bills on Cory's desk. "Put this on my account, please," she called over her shoulder as she dashed out of the door.

Whoever had abandoned Ashley had left her with some cash.

Cory wondered about the absence of any art materials in the place where Ashley had awakened. Were they removed? If so, why? Did she have a separate studio?

⤝ 3 ⤞

A day had passed with only a few return calls received from colleagues. No local psychologist reported any blackmail threats. Everyone urged her to notify her malpractice insurance company.

She carefully edited and posted an e-mail message on the psychology listserv:

> *Subject:* Blackmail
> *Message:* If you or a colleague experienced a blackmail threat from someone falsely claiming to be your patient, discussing this experience and results can be helpful and supportive. Let's share ideas for successful outcome.

She included her private email and phone numbers.

At the end of the day, five psychologists responded affirmatively to her private email address. A different company from Cory's insured three. All five had experienced the same scenario several years ago. None had paid blackmail and none were summoned to court. All were given excellent legal counseling from their malpractice insurance companies.

Relieved, she called her professional insurance agency, and was treated to quick and efficient service—a promise that an attorney would call her within the day. It was only mid-day on the east coast where the legal section was based. She gave her mobile phone number to the insurance agency.

Cory could prove the bogus patient had set her up by making and breaking an appointment two years ago.

She had an additional option. She could attempt to gather evidence from the five psychologists who prevailed in a similar situation. It seemed likely the litigant could have been the same bogus patient. She realized the difficulty in making this happen. Few would be willing to open old wounds and the blackmailer may have used different identities. Still, if necessary, it could be worth pursuing.

Cory habitually responded to injustices with appropriate measures, often to her satisfaction. Her first psychoanalyst, a rigid, pompous person, called her "an injustice collector." He noted she was always on the lookout for causes to join, and diagnosed it a sign of neurotic behavior. Cory regarded that aspect of her personality as one that defined her in a positive way. She chose not to change it. Instead, she changed her analyst. She had to provide a suitable reason to her supervisor for the change. She figured "a conflict of values" would suffice. And it did.

An hour later, Robert McGill, attorney for the insurance trust phoned her. She explained the situation, providing the facts.

"Doctor Cohen, please don't worry," McGill said in a strong, soothing, reassuring voice—the voice of someone experienced in commanding difficult situations. "We have two excellent attorneys in the San Diego area at your disposal. They will meet with you at your office tomorrow at your convenience. Let's set a time."

"The earlier, the better. Will nine work for them?" she asked.

"Yes. I'm sure that will be fine. You're the client, Doctor Cohen. We are here to serve you. From what you described, it is doubtful the case will be brought to court."

"That is reassuring, Mister McGill."

"However, if you were summoned to court, rest assured, your attorney would appear in your defense."

"Mister McGill, if I can prove the same person had attempted such a hoax before, what would the authorities do with a national blackmail scheme on their hands?"

"That is not our concern. I cannot advise you on that. It is the province of the assorted authorities."

"Thank you and goodbye for now," Cory muttered,

She hoped the culprit would soon be delivered, charged, and sent to prison. Carole Roy had probably caused her attempted blackmail victims sleepless nights and trying days.

Cory knew how that felt. She had experienced such a condition recently during Ben's unexpected long absence.

She never questioned her competence and her ability to get along well without a mate, yet she had begun to feel incomplete without Ben. She missed his comforting and enjoyable company. Their relationship had grown stronger since they began working together on his investigations, most recently in the U.K. where he had connections.

She had proved to be a clever, strong, and assertive partner and Ben had welcomed those attributes. Although they were independent, strong-willed people, they rarely butt heads. They loved the excitement, joy, and comfort of working and living together after many years of independence.

Cory was content with her current lifestyle—her offspring launched, managing mostly on their own, and Ben making no demands on her time. She had the freedom to choose her work and play schedules, but there were times when she yearned for the comfort of Ben's presence. Lately, those times came at a greater frequency.

Ben was investigating a private matter in the U.K. and hadn't called in over ten days. This was uncharacteristic of him and it worried her.

She grabbed her mobile phone and keyed in his long international number, eager to hear his soothing baritone voice, but he was unavailable.

Frustrated, and deeply concerned, she sent him a text requesting a call.

To relieve her tension, she changed into running clothes and jogged toward the beach for a long run. Ashley's house was on a quiet street near shops and the beach, and a short detour from her usual path. Many of the houses were vacation rentals. A few were rented for the entire racing season.

In order to read the house numbers, Cory slowed her pace to a walk. She located Ashley's quaint cottage surrounded by a surprisingly unkempt garden—as though careless movers had dragged the contents of the house across the garden, tearing up plants in the process.

She was surprised to see a printed sign posted on the gate:

PRIVATE SALE BY OWNER. NO BROKERS.

IF INTERESTED, LEAVE YOUR NAME

AND PHONE # UNDER THE FRONT DOOR.

Ashley hadn't mentioned the sign. Either she hadn't noticed it, or it was just posted.

Cory resisted the temptation to slide her card under the door. Her professional ethics would deem it unprofessional to play sleuth on behalf of a patient, no matter how well-intended.

And it was possible that tomorrow Ashley's memory would return and Cory's snooping would have been unnecessary.

She ran for forty minutes and returned to the office. After making a few notes, she tossed her planner and office clothes into her sport-bag and locked up.

With Ashley's amnesia upfront in her thoughts, she walked home eager to take a soothing shower.

Suddenly, she recalled the terrifying shower scene in *Psycho*. Long after the film had been released, many women still reported a fear of showering at home alone. Cory wasn't easily frightened, but she imagined how difficult it could be for someone who feels vulnerable—like Ashley. Cory couldn't get the young woman's plight out of her mind.

After a quick shower, she wrapped herself in her warm and cozy terry robe. Seated at her laptop, she Googled Ashley Hogan's name and located eighteen in California. Most had photos. None bore even a slight resemblance to her new patient. If Ashley were a professional artist, she would probably have a website. Either she was an amateur or used an alias for her work. Or perhaps her talent had not yet been discovered.

Soon it was bedtime and she still hadn't heard from Ben.

⸗ 4 ⸗

In the past, no matter where Ben landed, he wouldn't let more than a few days pass without calling Cory—especially if she had left him a message; thus her concern grew. Despite his repeated assurances to her about his work, she knew any investigation could include some danger. She tried to console herself that Ben was highly experienced and he had exercised more caution since their relationship had become serious. Repeatedly, he had mentioned that he was no longer willing to take on dangerous work. He had confidence that the London gig would be a relatively easy matter, requiring more of his technical skill than footwork.

Was he so consumed by work that he didn't think about her as much as she did about him? If she had a full practice, she may not have thought about Ben as often. Idleness was her enemy.

It was time for a distraction. She hauled out her bongos, turned on a bossa nova CD, and drummed. The music blocked the ringing of the phone. When she heard Ben leaving a message, she grabbed the phone.

"Ben, I'm here," she said, breathlessly.

"How are you, my sweet?" he asked

"Everything is fine except for my worrying about you."

"Sorry. I was out of reach. But I'm back in London now and I hope to be home soon."

Cory smiled. "Great. I miss you."

"Miss you, too, Cory. Anything going on you want to tell me? "

"Yes. I have a puzzling patient. An amnesia victim. She signed a release for you. Please let me know if Ashley P. Hogan, age twenty-two of California, is on the FBI radar screen or other useful database."

"I'll get on it as soon as possible and promise to let you know. I miss my sweetie."

"Miss you, too," she said.

She felt mildly relieved to hear him say they would soon be together. She couldn't put her finger on why she was only mildly relieved. Was it because of the unusual brevity of the conversation? She sensed something was amiss, but she had no evidence. Was their relationship too good to last?

"Stop torturing yourself. You deserve each other. It's the best relationship you've ever had," she whispered to herself.

Cory resumed drumming to the end of the CD. Feeling better, she dressed for the office and looked forward to Mimi's call with the results of Ashley's examination.

Clouds rolled in as Cory's boots hit the pavement on her way to work. A damp breeze blew her hair over her face. It wasn't the weather one expects on the San Diego coast, but it was after all, June Gloom, the month of intermittent gray skies and cooler temperatures. The scent of blooming Jasmine reminded her that it was the summer season, after all.

At the corner, she passed hedges of sweet-smelling Texas Privet, reminiscent of the blossoms surrounding the Brooklyn apartment house of her childhood.

As she approached Ashley's house, again she was tempted to slide her card under the door, but chickened out. Perhaps she could find the information on a real estate website, or ask her neighbor Rita, a realtor. Hopefully, she wouldn't have to do any of that because Ashley would recover her memory soon.

Cory was trained in hypnosis. It worked well for patients concerned with locating their misplaced objects, or patients in physical pain. Accident and crime victims were often able to recall important information through hypnosis.

If Ashley received a clean bill of health and hadn't yet recovered her memory, hypnosis could be useful. If Ashley proved a good subject, she could recover bits and pieces of her past. In time, she would put them together like a jigsaw puzzle.

Lost in thought, Cory arrived at the office, half-expecting to see Ann, her office manager and good friend. Wishful thinking, she told herself. She was happy Ann was in the midst of accomplishing her professional goals, but she missed her.

They had shared several traumatic experiences unexpected in a psychotherapy practice, and had become close friends. Now, her dear friend was very busy establishing her own professional life, three thousand miles away.

If Ann remembered Ashley Hogan and had any information about her, it would be a great service. She planned to call her after meeting with the attorneys.

At nine o'clock, two young, well-groomed, neatly attired attorneys—John Adams and Ron Stone—arrived at her office. They were assigned to her case from her malpractice insurance to discuss the blackmail threat.

Ron Stone, the taller of the two, reassured her that they had experience with this type of matter. They expected her worries would vanish since she had not replied to the blackmailer, and acted appropriately by contacting the insurance company. The blackmailer had no credible evidence to support ever being Doctor Cohen's patient.

"Couldn't the blackmailer print up a fake receipt on the computer, listing my name and address, the date, the procedure code, and fee for service?" she asked.

"Sure she could. Anyone can. But she can't prove it's a valid receipt. She wouldn't be able to provide her cancelled check written to you, and if she said she paid in cash, she would not have any proof of the transaction."

Mildly relieved, Cory sighed. She related an incident she observed in court when she heard a judge accept false evidence. Cory knew for a fact that the evidence was absolutely untrue.

"Yes. That can happen, but with an attorney representing you, you will be protected," John Adams said.

They advised her to notify them at once should she be summoned to court, and assured her they would proceed in appropriate fashion. Again, they counseled her to do nothing unless she received anything related to the matter. In such a case, as they told her, she must call them immediately. They provided her with their business cards, listing a La Jolla office address and phone number, and assured her they were at her disposal.

"Thank you for coming here and reassuring me. You're fine gentlemen, but I hope I won't have to see you again—at least not in these circumstances." A bit flirtatious, perhaps, but a compliment nonetheless.

Cory turned her attention to her current work. She clicked on the contact list on her mobile and called Ann's current phone number. It was a little after one o'clock in the afternoon on the east coast. Ann did not pick up the call. Cory left a message.

~ 5 ~

The morning of her hair donation appointment was cool and cloudy-- suitable for wearing her black leather jacket, black jeans, cap, and boots—her "tough looking lady" apparel.

She was about to step into her car, when she remembered that Ben had asked her to drive his car for at least fifteen minutes a few times a week to keep the battery charged. Having forgotten to do it last week, she felt a pang of guilt. If she mentioned her lapse to Joe, her dear friend, a psychoanalyst, he would have correctly asked her why she was angry with Ben.

Having driven to Wigs for Kids many times, she knew it would take about twenty minutes in moderate traffic on the freeway. The trip would meet her obligation to Ben. She opened the glove compartment in his black luxurious Lexus and removed his car keys.

Cory's calculations were accurate. She arrived a few minutes early and found a parking space in front of Healthy Touch Massage Salon a few doors away from her destination.

Fifteen minutes later, she emerged with her hair ten inches shorter, a smile of satisfaction, and ample time before work.

Wind whipped around her as she hastened down the street toward Ben's car, keys in her hand ready to open the car door. Suddenly, she heard the blast of a gun. The sound, so close to her ear, was unmistakable.

Shaken, she dashed toward the door of the massage salon. Just as she opened it, another shot rang out, shattering the glass above the door.

"Lady, drop to floor," the Asian proprietor screamed, her phone in hand. "Come quick. Gun shots," she shouted into the phone. "You have the address. No one hurt bad inside. Don't know outside."

On her elbows and knees, grateful for the padded protection of her clothes, Cory crawled on the floor, trying to avoid the shards of glass as she approached the middle of the jade-green carpeted waiting room. Feeling safer inside the confines of the salon, she stood on her shaky feet and thanked the proprietor.

"Blood on hand. I fix," the proprietor said. Reaching under the counter, she withdrew a first aid kit and a small white towel. "Come," she commanded. She spread a newspaper on the floor, and moistened the towel.

"Stand here," she pointed to the newspaper.

Cory obeyed. The woman delicately dabbed the wet cloth over pieces of glass detaching them from Cory's clothes onto the cloth and newspaper.

"Give me hand. I look." Gently, she squeezed the wound, emitting a few drops of blood. "Not deep. It okay." She poured a dollop of baby shampoo on the small, bloody wound, and patted it with a sterile gauze pad before affixing a large Band-Aid. "You lucky. No need stitches."

Grateful for the woman's kind attention, Cory smiled and thanked her.

"Lady, how 'bout massage, make you feel better, calm you? We do after police go?"

Cory shook her head. "Sorry, I have to work today. Do you hear gunshots often in this neighborhood?"

"One time, two year past," the woman replied. Why they after you? Why you, good Asian woman like me? What you do wrong?"

"I don't know!" Cory shouted over the nearby police siren.

Two officers entered the salon and interviewed Cory, the proprietor, and the massage therapist. Apparently there was no one else was in the small salon.

Upon questioning, Cory explained her mission in the neighborhood.

"Commendable," said an officer. "How soon after you left your donation were the shots fired?"

"The first one occurred when I was just a few steps away from Wigs for Kids, approaching my car. The second shot rang out almost immediately afterwards in front of this place."

Do you know of anyone who may want to hurt you?" The officer asked.

"No. I don't think I was the target."

"From where you heard the first shot, it is very likely you were the target. It's obvious that the last shot was aimed at you."

Considering her precarious existence, Cory shuddered.

She found it difficult to focus on answering his queries about where she lived, worked, and the nature of her work.

"Maybe I was mistaken for someone else," she said, hoping it was the truth.

The policeman gave her a sideways glance and shook his head.

Cory's thoughts raced. Did Ashley have an enemy who figured Cory knew too much? Was Cory targeted because of what the enemy thought Ashley revealed to her?

Wouldn't Ashley be a more appropriate target?

Or, was Ben's car a target for someone who wanted to hurt or warn him to comply with a demand? Was this incident a portent of more danger ahead?

Perhaps the shooting had nothing to do with Ashley or Ben.

Cory had no idea why she, a low-profile psychologist was a target. She preferred to consider it a case of mistaken identity.

Her thoughts flashed back to Carole Roy, the attempted blackmailer. In the absence of any further action on the bogus case, Cory figured that the letter-writer had given up on the frivolous lawsuit.

Cory could not believe any legitimate lawyer would accept a weak case without adequate evidence to substantiate that a relationship had existed between a specific doctor and patient. The "patient/ litigant" would not be able to produce a valid cancelled check, or receipt for payment of an office visit. Fees to bring the case to court would cost more than the requested five thousand dollars.

But a receipt could be falsified by printing one out on a computer, or she could say she paid in cash. The cash part would weaken the already poor case.

It seemed unreasonable that after two years, and a single session with a psychologist, a patient would come to the conclusion she, or he, was a victim of malpractice by that psychologist—and would be believed.

But then again, just because payment wasn't made doesn't mean that a session wasn't provided. What if her confidential records were summoned?

Well, she'd call her malpractice attorney to prevent such a scenario.

Cory knew that paranoid, delusional people held such beliefs for a lifetime, but she consoled herself by figuring the attempt on her life was probably connected to Ashley.

Cory decided at this point sharing her concerns about Ashley with the police wasn't appropriate; better to protect a fragile patient from police involvement. By now, Ashley was safely ensconced in the confines of a cheery hotel.

"Get that door fixed immediately. It's dangerous," the officer barked at the proprietor.

"I do. Call insurance lady today."

"You need to call right away. Sweep up the shards, now," the officer demanded.

"May I leave now?" Cory asked.

He nodded, handing her his card and a list of resources for victims of violence. "I hope you won't need this," he said.

"We'll contact you if necessary. If you think of anything to help our investigation, please call."

"I appreciate your quick response," Cory said.

She turned to the proprietor and hugged her. "You're very kind. Thanks," she said.

"You good. No afraid. Come for massage, soon."

Cory grabbed a card from the counter, and smiled at the caring woman for whom she felt an odd attachment—as if she were a long-lost relative.

For a brief moment, Cory wondered whether her life would have been much different if an Asian mother had raised her instead of a Jewish grandmother.

Compassion has nothing to do with ethnicity, she thought.

* * *

With great caution, Cory drove from the massage salon to her office, frequently checking her rear and side view mirrors.

She realized she would have felt safer if a police officer had escorted her home. She should have asked. Given that she wasn't a Very Important Person, it was unlikely her request would have been granted, but she should have tried. No, the damsel–in–distress role wasn't her style.

After her rape and near-death experience more than a dozen years ago, Cory had earned a karate black belt. It heightened her self-confidence and lessened her feelings of vulnerability, but she realized that martial arts could not protect her in every dangerous situation.

Cory parked in her usual space near the door to her office, happy to be alive, but still rattled from her misadventure.

The salon proprietor's kind, hasty attention comforted her. Gratitude demanded more than a quick hug.

She retrieved the card from Healthy Touch Massage Salon, whipped out her credit card, and opened her laptop. She ordered a large bouquet of the freshest mixed flowers in a jade-colored glass vase to be sent to the salon. She directed the card to read: "Many thanks for your quick thinking, kindness, and protection." Someone more articulate in English than the proprietor, perhaps a bilingual child, would translate it in the good woman's native tongue.

≈ 6 ≈

Because Cory's diminished schedule allowed time for community service, she had registered for pro bono work. Today, she was grateful for the distraction. Her first such patient was Elena.

Elena arrived disheveled, barefoot, and ten minutes late. *Ambivalence about therapy is often the cause of lateness*, remembered Cory, but she resolved to reserve judgment.

"I couldn't find parking is why I'm late," Elena blurted.

"I'm sorry. I should have mentioned the reserved parking spaces in my driveway."

Elena glared at Cory. "Yeah, you should have, instead of making me look hard for parking."

"I apologized."

"Yeah, I heard you, lady."

Elena's confrontational style, her anger and rudeness were misplaced. Such overreactions usually caused discomfort to those on the receiving end, and Cory was no exception.

"We've just met. Surely, you can't be this angry with me, after I apologized. Which person in your life makes you most angry?"

"That's easy. My man Lonnie. We been tight a long time, but he's no good no more. He's been cheating on me."

"Are you sure?" Cory asked.

"Don't you believe me?"

"I don't know you well enough yet," Cory admitted.

"Well, I got proof on his email. He makes dates with his ole girlfriend—the Ho. He sneaks out for sex with her every damn day."

"You confronted him?" Cory asked

"What you mean?"

"You told him you know about it?"

Elena nodded. "He says I'm nuts."

"Did you show him proof?"

"I tried, but he deleted his email."

"What would you like to do about it?" Cory asked.

Elena's eyes blazed. "Kill him. Scratch her eyes out," she yelled.

"How would you kill him?"

"Drugs. He does drugs big time. I could slip him something real bad." Elena grinned, like a mischievous child.

"But you take drugs, too."

"So what if I do?" Elena yelled.

"Do drugs get you in trouble?" Cory asked.

"Sure do. A week ago, we was snatched for disturbing the peace. When Lonnie and me gets mad, we beat up on each other. Damn nosey neighbors call the cops. Sometime, we wine up in jail overnight to cool us off. Once, I get so mad, I stab him and he done bleed real bad. An ambulance took him to the hospital and the cops tossed me in the slammer!"

Given Elena's unbridled anger, propensity for violence, and drug abuse, Cory worried about what she had gotten herself into with pro-bono work. Having experienced more danger in her professional life than most psychologists, she should have been specific in the cases she would take. Drug addiction was not up her alley. She'd try to help Elena with another problem.

"Would you like to learn how to control yourself so that no one gets hurt?" Cory asked.

"I jes wanna make him stop doin' it with that ho."

"I'm sorry, but I can't help you with that, Elena."

"Den what I done come here foe?" She stood, eyes blazing, her hands on her hips.

"Elena, I'm trying to help you in other ways. Maybe we can figure out why you stay with Lonnie when he cheats on you. Cory motioned her to sit. Elena obliged.

"What do you get from him?" Cory asked.

"All the drugs I want."

"Are drugs worth the price of feeling hurt and angry over his girlfriend?"

"He, he, he, hah," Elena laughed as though tickled by a feather. "No ma'am. I need my drugs more den I need my man."

"Elena, I hope you realize that nothing will change until you're ready to get help for your dependence on drugs—and on Lonnie," Cory said.

"Spose so. Maybe I gotta think bout it more."

"Yes. You can start to make healthy choices."

"You mean I gotta buy me that crap frozen food?"

Restraining a laugh, Cory smiled.

"You makin fun of me?" Elena glared.

Elena was perceptive and hypersensitive. Illicit drugs probably served to shield her from the sting of emotional blows.

"Oh, I'm sorry, Elena. I wasn't talking about food. I meant making good choices for your life. I don't make fun of people."

"So you say. I don't trust you. You could tell the cops bout Lonnie and me selling drugs."

"That isn't my job, and the police know about it from when they hauled you off to jail. My job is to help you to make your life better, but you must want the kind of help I offer. Taking drugs may make you feel good for a time, but they have bad consequences."

Elena crossed her arms over her chest. "So how you gonna make my life better if I don't have Lonnie and I don't have drugs neither?"

"Have you ever attended an N.A. meeting?"

"Huh?" Elena looked puzzled.

"O.K. Just a second," Cory said. She rummaged through her files and whipped out a handout sheet from Narcotics Anonymous and handed it to Elena.

"It explains the purpose of the organization and lists local meetings," Cory said.

Elena scanned the list. "I ain't quitting, and I ain't going to no church," she shouted.

"These groups help thousands of former addicts. You would experience the benefits of quitting drugs. No more trouble with cops. No dependence on Lonnie, and you'll be healthier."

Noticing Elena mouthing "blah, blah, blah," Cory stopped the harangue, and shook her head. She decided that further efforts to convince this woman would be futile.

"I'm fine. I dig gettin' high," Elena chuckled. "I ain't gonna give it up no-way. Besides, Lonnie and me makes a lot selling." She gasped, covered her hand over her mouth. "Uh-oh! You gonna tell on me. I know it." Elena's eyes blazed.

"Our session is confidential. The police already know about the drugs. Weren't you high when they picked you up?"

"Yeah," Elena nodded.

"My job is to help you become healthier, but I can't help you until you decide to quit drugs."

Elena stood and waved a sheet of paper in Cory's face. "Jess sign dis dam paper to show I was here."

Cory complied.

Elena grabbed the paper, muttered something that sounded like a curse as Cory escorted her to the front door.

≈ 7 ≈

After the unrewarding session with Elena, Cory felt relieved to see her longtime patient Larry seated in the waiting room.

"Hi, Doc. Good to see you."

Cory smiled. "How come you're so early today?"

"Working at home now, I manage my time more efficiently. My co-workers can't interrupt me asking me to stop what I'm doing to help them with their work."

A passive man, Larry had found a way to avoid saying "No."

"Your boss will notice how valuable you are."

Larry was a brilliant man, devoted to his engineering career. He instinctively knew how mechanical things worked, but he needed to feel better about himself, to stand up to those who would take advantage of him. Larry was in treatment with Cory for two years. Progress was slow, but both felt it was worth the baby steps he'd taken.

At forty-five, he was single and longed for, but never had a long-time relationship. Sadly, he hadn't connected with a woman who would accept more than a second date with him. Cory wished she could see him in action to determine how to help him fix his problem. She had tried role-playing with him, but it didn't help. She had put the word out to colleagues for an appropriate therapy group for him.

Larry craved a relationship with a woman who would respect him and wouldn't take advantage of his passivity as many of his colleagues had done. He had registered on online dating services, but rarely had more than one date with the same woman.

Larry was a pleasant looking man, tall and lean, with short black hair, trimmed beard, large brown eyes, and a wide smile. A marathon runner, he was in good physical shape, helpful, and good-natured. Despite all of his attributes, he hadn't yet made a suitable connection.

"I have some good news. I ran into a fine young woman. She's much younger than me, but quite mature. We met while we were standing at the end of a long line at the San Diego Art Museum last Sunday. We walked around together, viewing the paintings. She was easy to talk to and she loves art. I took her to dinner at the Prado and she invited me to a reception at a gallery in La Jolla next Saturday. I could hardly wait to tell you."

Larry's good news brightened Cory's day. She smiled and applauded him.

"I'm counting the days until I see Ashley, again."

Cory broke out in goose bumps. It would be a remarkable coincidence if Larry had connected with Ashley Hogan.

"What do you know about Ashley, Larry?"

"She didn't talk much about herself, mostly about the paintings we were looking at. She did say that she lives in Del Mar and is grad student in Art History at U.C.S.D."

"Did she mention her last name?"

"No, she didn't, but she gave me her phone number." He reached into his pocket to search for her number on his phone.

"Have you called her yet?"

"I just met her a few days ago. I don't want to look too eager. Do you think I should call her tonight?"

"It may be a good idea to confirm your meeting."

"You're right. I'm no good at this dating game."

"Dating isn't a game, although some people have bad experiences with online dating services and they think the people they meet are playing games. It may be because they expect to meet their ideal mate and are disappointed when it doesn't work out.

"You met Ashley in the best way—easy and natural. Two people meet unexpectedly and enjoy each other's company. You deserve a new friend. Before your next session, I'd like to know how your phone call went."

If the phone were disconnected, Cory would deal with Larry's disappointment.

In the proper hands, the number could offer a clue to resurrect the calling history if the young woman turned out to be Ashley Hogan.

If Larry made contact, it would be all the better for him.

≈ 8 ≈

Cory had not heard from Ashley all day. Perhaps she was busy with the tests Mimi had set up for her. She picked up the phone and reached Mimi. "Any news about Ashley?"

"I just finished for the day and was about to phone you. Bottom line. Ashley appears to be in excellent physical condition. She had a thorough workup. No evidence of any injury or tumor. The blood and urine samples will take a few more days, but I don't expect any surprise. In my opinion, the cause of her amnesia is psychogenic. She's in good hands with you, Cory. Thanks for referring her."

"I appreciate your thoroughness, Mimi. Did you give her the results?"

"Yes. She called me for them a few hours ago. She wasn't entirely relieved with the news. She seemed to expect we'd find a tumor that would be easily removed and she would instantly regain her memory. Amazing how naïve some people are."

"I know. Some think, like insurance companies pretend—that I can perform magic in a few sessions. Did she tell you her plans?"

"She settled into a hotel and plans to continue with you."

"This will be a challenging case for me and I need one right now."

"Want to talk about it over a glass of wine and dinner at Pacifica? I saw you walking to your office this morning. I could pick you up now and drive you home later."

Pleased with Mimi's suggestion, Cory agreed.

Two years ago, after Mimi Green had moved into the medical building adjacent to Cory's office, she had invited Cory to a reception for the opening of her internal medicine practice. Subsequently, they had become friends. Both were divorced and empty nesters. Mimi's children were attending Ivy League universities. An avid reader, she loved to discuss the current book she was reading. It was usually one Cory had heard about on Books TV, but hadn't found the time to read. Mimi could be described as the quintessential high I.Q. bookworm and an excellent, caring physician. Cory enjoyed her intellectually stimulating conversation.

Pacifica Del Mar had spectacular ocean views. Perched atop the Del Mar Plaza, the well-prepared food and service made it a popular meeting place.

The two women preferred sitting at a small table on the terrace overlooking the ocean, watching the sunset to the intense social scene at the bar.

Suddenly, their attention was drawn to a fashionably dressed, attractive young woman standing with a man, yelling at him, "Don't you dare tell him, or I'll... I'll get even with you."

Quickly, the manager left his post near the entry and rushed over to the woman, calmly ushering her outside. He appeared to know her. He spoke with her for a few moments until she calmed down. Cory watched him escort the woman to the elevator before returning to his post.

"What was that all about?" Mimi whispered.

"The guy threatened to tell her husband about something that would hurt her."

"I figured that out, but what do you think it was?" Mimi asked.

"Could be she lost money on an investment, or at the track, or is romantically involved with someone other than her husband."

"Or the guy is her drug dealer," Mimi offered.

"As if we don't have enough excitement from our patients." Cory frowned.

"I invited you here to relax, Cory. You're unusually tense."

"Astute, Doctor Green."

"Want to talk about it? I'm not a shrink, but I am your friend."

"And I appreciate that, Mimi." Cory paused. She wasn't comfortable sharing her feelings about Ben with Mimi. Mimi was not a romantic. She was pure science and probably wouldn't understand.

"I miss seeing more patients. My practice is a big part of me," Cory said.

"I understand. I always refer appropriate patients to you," Mimi offered.

The server brought the wine in generous-sized wine glasses.

"I appreciate your confidence in me," Cory held up her wineglass. "Cheers."

They clicked glasses. "I'm also not as busy as I'd like," Mimi said. "This is a desirable area and many new docs are opening up practices here. There is an abundance of medical facilities and still more under construction."

"But the new docs have to gain a reputation, which you already enjoy." Cory smiled.

"Thanks for your trust. I'd rather treat patients than do anything else. My work has always been consuming, so much so that it interfered with my marriage. My husband had more leisure time as a professor than I did. He liked to travel frequently, but I regarded it as a huge inconvenience, so we went our separate ways."

Cory was pleased that Mimi had opened up to her.

"He didn't agree with your priorities."

"I refused to change and have no regrets."

"Mimi, is your work your highest priority?"

"Absolutely, I'm happier now than ever."

"You are a remarkable, self-contained person." Cory had thought she, too, was self-contained until Ben entered her life.

On a warm late afternoon, Pacifica was crowded. After they had drained their wine glasses, they were ready for dinner. Cory had not yet heard from Ashley or Ben.

Mimi was a fine dinner companion. Conversation flowed easily and was usually about intellectual matters, rarely about feelings. Cory enjoyed the interlude. The two women had very different personalities, but both shared a passion for their work.

When Cory arrived home, she found a package at her door from her daughter Rachel. Unwrapping the package, she smiled. Rachel had located Cory's favorite imported licorice candy and shipped it to her. "You made my day brighter, Rachael," she whispered.

Because it was too late to call her, she sent an email message. Unable to resist checking the in-box, she clicked on a message from Ben:

Miss you. Nothing on the AH matter.

If he could send an email, he could make a call. Why hadn't he?

She went to bed frustrated, but the large glass of wine had made her groggy and she fell asleep easily.

⚯ 9 ⚯

Cory tried to put Ashley's challenging situation to rest. Without the young woman's presence, there was nothing she could do on her behalf. Perhaps Ashley had already recovered her memory and no longer needed help. It would be thoughtful if she notified Cory, but closure for Cory was her issue, not the patient's.

Unlike earlier years, this was an era when many patients wanted a quick fix, and polite behavior wasn't always a priority. Not fully invested in psychotherapy, some simply abandoned it without saying goodbye.

Cory realized that she should consider her own personal well-being. Would she be safer if Ashley were not her patient, assuming the gun shot incident was connected to Ashley?

It was too late for that. If the shooter thought she knew too much about Ashley, stopping therapy wouldn't make a difference.

Since Ashley hadn't reported any threats against her, perhaps Cory had been targeted for another reason.

The ringing of her mobile phone interrupted her musings.

Mimi was calling from her private line. "I need a break. Do you have a few minutes to meet me on the patio at L'Auberge?"

"Is something wrong, Mimi? Why not meet at your office or mine?

"I'll explain in person," Mimi replied.

Cory locked her office, and rushed to meet Mimi.

* * *

"I needed some fresh air. It's been a wild day. Now, what I'm about to tell you may have to do with Ashley.

"After dropping you off last night, I realized I had been closely followed by a car. At first I thought it was a coincidence—a local resident driving from the Del Mar Plaza garage to your street and then to my street. From my rear view mirror, the driver appeared to be a woman.

"No sooner had I parked the car in my garage, the doorbell rang. Naturally, I wouldn't open the door for a stranger. I asked who she was and what she wanted.

"She identified herself as Lydia Brooks, a private investigator. She placed a card outside the window panel near my front door. The card listed her as Chief Officer Discrete Investigation Service in Phoenix.

"She said she had an important message for the woman I had recently dropped off. She had tried to deliver it, but no one answered the doorbell. She caught up with me at the traffic signal and followed me home, hoping I'd convey her message to you.

"I found myself unnerved by this disconcerting incident. I told her to stop bothering me or I'd call 911. As she drove off, I tried to read her license number, but it was impossible to read it at night. What do you make of this?"

Cory shrugged. "I really don't know. It certainly is odd. Probably, I didn't hear the doorbell because my radio was on."

"If she wanted to speak with you, she wasn't very clever. All she had to do is look you up online, find your phone number, and call it. Surely, even a novice investigator would know that," Mimi said.

"Yes, Mimi, but she probably experienced a lot of failures in her attempts to interview people on the phone. Catching them in person probably works better."

"I can understand that, Cory, but I'm a very private person and felt invaded by her. In retrospect, perhaps I was too harsh with her. Anyway, I thought you should know."

"Thanks for reporting this to me Mimi. That detective or whoever she is must have seen us together. It means someone is watching me."

"How bizarre! Why?"

Cory shrugged. "Perhaps it's the company I keep."

Mimi grimaced. "Is that supposed to be funny, Cory?"

"Sorry, Mimi. It's a bad joke."

Cory reflected on the gunshot incident and was about to share it with Mimi, but decided not to hold up a danger sign in front of their friendship.

"Please be careful, Cory. You may have a paranoid or psychopath among your patients."

"Not currently, but you're right. Such folks may store imaginary hurt for years before acting on it. Thanks for telling me, Mimi. Let's have lunch soon. Please pick a place and phone when it's convenient."

The two women rose from the patio chairs, and hurried back to their respective offices.

Cory wondered about a possible connection between the shooting outside the salon and the "investigator."

She hurried back to her office, seated herself in front of her laptop, and Googled "Discreet Investigations" She hurried to finish before Tom, a new patient arrived.

There were several listings for that name located in various cities, but none in Phoenix.

The "investigator" had a common name. Perhaps it was an alias. Anyone could create a calling card using false information. It would be futile to find the woman who had shadowed Mimi.

An amateur, she figured. But why would someone check on her? She was not a public figure and she kept a low profile.

She felt respected by those who knew her and found it hard to believe she had any enemies. Was she wrong?

The shooting, the possibly bogus private investigator, and Mimi's concern drew her to re-examine the few paranoid patients that had visited her office.

Given a success rate of zero with paranoids, she had declined treating such patients long ago.

The only scenario that made any sense connecting the shooting and the private investigator was Ashley's trauma.

If the trauma that precipitated Ashley's amnesia was of a criminal nature, it was possible the perpetrator would want Ashley to remain in the dark forever; but harming, killing, or threatening Ashley's therapist would not be the most effective measure. Ashley would have to be the victim, not Cory, unless somehow Cory was mistaken for Ashley. That was highly unlikely, as they bore no resemblance to each other whatsoever.

Although the two unnerving incidents could be related, she preferred to believe that the shooter had mistaken her for someone else—identity unknown.

Frustrated with the puzzle, she cast it aside, and opened the door to greet her new patient Tom, arriving five minutes early.

The productive session improved her spirits and gave Tom some hope of salvaging his tarnished marriage to an unfaithful wife. He had erectile dysfunction and had refused to meet his wife's request that he take medication to improve their sex life. Tom took responsibility for his failure to please his wife sexually and vowed to explore other ways to satisfy her.

Just as he walked out the door, Ann phoned.

"What's up?" Ann asked.

"First tell me how you're doing, Ann."

"My boss, the professor is awesome. It's a pleasure to work with him."

"You sound ecstatic, Ann. I'm glad it's working out well for you."

"I think I'm really cut out for research."

"Ann, you could do practically anything well."

"Is that your professional opinion?"

"Absolutely. Listen, I'm sorry to interrupt your work, but I have a question. Do you recall meeting Ashley Hogan when you were here? She has my card with your name scrawled on the back."

"That's odd. I don't remember her. Why is it important? What's going on, Cory?"

"She has amnesia and I'm trying to help her regain her memory. She may have witnessed a traumatic event."

"Describe her."

"She's young, petite, pale complexion, light brown or blondish hair, fashioned in a bun, small brown eyes, well-dressed. She may be a professional artist. She lives in a cottage near the beach in Del Mar."

"I'm drawing a blank, but I'll dredge my memory bank and call you if something surfaces."

"I appreciate that. I miss you and I'm happy for you."

≈ 10 ≈

Later that day, Tom's infidel wife Susan called Cory for an appointment "the sooner, the better." They scheduled it for six that evening.

Ashley called shortly before six. "Sorry, I didn't get back to you sooner. I was busy moving into a charming bed and breakfast in Cardiff. Lots of antiques and a wood burning fireplace." She rambled on as though amnesia was no longer a problem until Cory interrupted. "Have you remembered anything, Ashley?"

"Some vague things. Like the place where I've checked in. It feels like home to me, not like a hotel at all. Either I've been here before, or somewhere similar. Homey, and comfortable. I knew exactly where the dining room was located at the end of a long hallway. I also expected my room would be like a studio apartment with a refrigerator and micro."

"Many places have those amenities, Ashley, but maybe you really were there before. Did the staff recognize you?"

"Funny, you should ask. They seemed familiar to me, but they acted like I was a newcomer, so maybe I wasn't there before."

"The area is flooded with tourists. It may be hard for staff to remember every former guest. When it's quiet at the desk, ask if they have a record of your previous visit. Many hotels keep registrations on a computer file to offer specials or discounts to former guests."

"I'll do that," Ashley said.

Cory glanced at the wall clock. Susan would arrive any minute. "Sorry, Ashley, I must cut this short. Let's get together tomorrow morning. Would ten work for you?"

Ashley sighed. "I'm scared to go to Del Mar. Someone there may be after me. Please meet me at the Cardiff Inn."

"I understand. I don't usually make house calls, but under the circumstances, I'll make an exception. Give me the address, and I'll be there at ten."

Cory jotted down the address just as the bell rang. The security video revealed a very attractive young woman who looked familiar. Cory buzzed in Tom's remorseful wife, Susan.

At the end of the session, as Susan pranced out the door, Cory realized she was the woman who had created a scene at Pacifica. This was a small town after all.

≠11≠

In preparation for her visit to the Cardiff Inn to meet with Ashley, Cory formulated a tentative treatment plan. Ashley had experienced a trauma horrendous enough to cause amnesia. Calling it to the surface too soon would be wrong. The immediate goal was to comfort and support her and then to help her remember her early life, her schooling, and her relationships, where she had lived—things that normal people recall with ease.

Ashley had mentioned that the Cardiff Inn seemed familiar to her. Perhaps she'd been there before. Likely, the innkeepers maintained a record of guests. Had the furnishings stirred memories of another place similar to it?

Since Ashley had likely witnessed a crime, it probably occurred where she had awakened.

The city of Del Mar issued weekly crime records in the local newspaper. The internet would provide such information. Cory knew the date and a likely location.

After extensive research she learned of three disorderly conduct citations on Camino del mar outside a popular bar on the evening before Ashley came to see her. Two robberies occurred at the Del Mar Fairgrounds. There were no violent crimes reported anywhere in the North County during the time period in question.

She had searched out of curiosity and the desire to help the young woman, but it was time-consuming and unproductive and not in her job description.

Cory wasn't a professional detective and Ben wasn't available. She felt dependent upon him, and uncomfortable about it. She yearned for his affection and needed his investigative skills. The case was difficult and she needed a distraction. No, that was a rationalization. She knew darn well that Ben would be on her mind no matter what was going on.

Conjuring up a few pleasant memories made her smile—like dessert after a fine meal.

Enough, she told herself. Time to focus on a treatment plan.

Hypnosis, combined with supportive and cognitive therapy, was the ticket for Ashley.

The short drive to the Inn along the Pacific Coast afforded a relaxing interlude, but concern over the shooting incident interfered. She decided to accept it as a case of mistaken identity.

Driving along the beach bought back pleasant memories of summertime at Brighton Beach along the Atlantic Ocean, her playground from childhood through high school. Fondly, she recalled family picnics, swimming, reading under an umbrella and noshing with gusto on "Mrs. Stahl's Knishes."

Ashley may have a favorite place, too. Perhaps it was also the beach. After all, she had found herself in a beach cottage before her first contact with Cory.

With impunity, Freud had treated some patients in a public park. A stickler for rules, Cory considered her out of office session—a stroll on the beach with her patient to be acceptable therapeutic behavior, given Freud's therapeutic milieu and Ashley's special circumstances.

She arrived at the Inn, a large building, reminiscent of a grand Cape Cod home. The parking lot contained a late-model, bright fire-engine red Lexus and an old white Mercedes, and a taxicab-yellow Honda. Cory pegged Ashley's car as one of the less flamboyant vehicles. Judging from her attire, she wasn't a flashy person and would likely prefer the older Mercedes.

Cory entered the ornate lobby reminiscent of a museum. Antique furniture and stunning silk tapestry wall hangings surrounded a massive stone fireplace. Oriental style rugs graced the floors. The ceilings were unusually high. At the reception desk, she asked for Ashley Hogan.

"Ashley is waiting for you in the breakfast room." The clerk pointed to the right.

Cory hurried down a long hallway.

They met halfway. "I hoped you'd have breakfast with me, here," Ashley said.

"Just coffee. Will we have undisturbed privacy?" Cory asked.

"Yes. I may be the only guest here now. It's quite comfortable and private and brighter in the breakfast room than anywhere else here."

"Okay, after breakfast, we can walk and talk on the beach or go back to your room—wherever you feel more comfortable."

Cory wished she had insisted on her office for this session. The atmosphere at the Inn wasn't conducive for hypnosis or for any kind of therapy. It seemed foreboding, like a haunted house, but Ashley said she found it comfortable. Perhaps she had known a similar environment that was pleasant for her. Would assessing Ashley's comfort level in different environments yield a memory?

They sat opposite each other over coffee and moist, chunky date-nut bread at a large wooden table suitable for six people.

"The hotel owner told me they have a sprinkle of guests here after Labor Day, but it's jammed the whole summer," Ashley said.

"I'd like our time together to be as helpful as possible to you, Ashley. Have you remembered anything from before amnesia set in?"

"Nothing at all. I'm glad to be here. The staff is friendly and helpful. The room comes with breakfast, and later in the day, they serve cheese and fruit and delicious muffins so I don't have to go out for dinner."

Ashley rambled on about the service, the food and antiques. It was clear that she was avoiding talking about amnesia. Perhaps she wished the lid on her memory would miraculously lift. She seemed nervous—afraid of what she may learn.

Various efforts to engage her were unproductive. Cory grew impatient and felt she was wasting time and energy.

Ashley may have sensed Cory's frustration. "This place is familiar to me. I've asked the owner if they have other hotels like this elsewhere and she said they don't. I also found out they keep registration records for seven years. I told her I had amnesia and that you would be visiting me here to help. We needed to know if I had ever stayed here. She said if you have something to identify yourself as a psychologist, she'll allow you to access the records."

"Ashley, that isn't a psychologist's job, but we'll talk to the owner together. I'll provide my credentials and ask her to allow you to do the research."

"Oh, I was planning on paying you to do it," Ashley said.

Cory's jaw dropped and her body stiffened from the surprisingly bold imposition. It gave her a new perspective of Ashley. The young woman behaved as a privileged person, with feelings of entitlement, ordering others to do her bidding. She had persuaded Cory to come to the hotel and now tried to manipulate her to search through musty old hotel registration books.

Was she naïve? Was she feigning amnesia? Why would she do so? Was she attempting to hide a crime? Until Cory found proof, she would go along with this possible charade—up to a point.

Cory suggested a stroll on the beach, hoping a change of scene would yield some result. Ashley reluctantly agreed.

During the walk, Cory tried to engage her in small talk, but Ashley seemed obsessed with the antiques at the Inn. She was convinced they were priceless and authentic, but couldn't substantiate her conviction.

When they returned to the hotel, Ashley introduced Cory to the owner. Upon request, Cory produced her driver's and psychology licenses. The owner agreed to allow Ashley to go through the registration books later that day.

"I'll take them to my room, now," Ashley demanded.

The owner's face reddened. She gave Ashley, a cold stare. "I'm doing you a favor, young lady. I have no time now to dig them up. You'll have to wait until later. For security reasons, you must use the desk inside the office. You mustn't make any notations. If you find what you're looking for, I'll let you copy it."

"Oh! Okay," Ashley stammered.

Abashed and surprised at Ashley's interaction with the hotel owner, Cory reluctantly followed her into her room.

After they were seated across from each other, Cory tried to use simple relaxation techniques to initiate a meditative mood. Her plan was to move on to hypnosis, but Ashley was resistant. She resumed talking about the antiques at the Inn. Why was she obsessed with them?

Cory asked Ashley to associate her feelings and thoughts about the furnishings, to try to imagine them at another place, but Ashley drew a blank.

Cory glanced at her Timex. She had spent over two hours with Ashley and was left with the feeling that either Ashley was a fraud or unsuitable for the kind of therapy Cory could provide.

There was another possibility. Ashley could have two distinct identities—a rare condition also known as "Dissociative Identity

Disorder", at one time categorized as "Multiple Personality Disorder."

Cory recalled that when they had first met, Ashley seemed to be a fragile person, terrified about not being able to remember her identity or a single thing from her past. After extensive medical exams, it was concluded that her amnesia stemmed from a psychological trauma. She had seemed desperate for help and appreciative of it.

Today, Ashley's manner was quite different. She was manipulative, obsessive, and evaded any therapeutic intervention. She seemed to take her amnesia in stride.

"I'm sorry, Ashley. I don't think I can help you, now."

"I don't understand. I thought you were my psychologist and would help me to remember."

"It seems you're not ready for my help."

Ashley pouted. "What should I do?"

"You could speak to a journalist from the local newspaper. Your amnesia would make a newsworthy item. A photographer would be assigned to take your photo. The headline would probably read something like "Do you know this woman?" or "Who is she?" The article would instruct any reader familiar with you to call the newspaper.

"Sometimes this kind of human-interest story is picked up by other news media. This would offer a greater chance of reaching someone who knows you to help fill in the blanks."

"But I know my identity. I'm Ashley Hogan."

"Yes, but details about yourself are currently missing from your memory. Someone may be able to help fill the void."

Ashley grimaced. "Oh, no! The idea of publicity scares me." She paused. "Well, at least I know something about my character. I'm a very private person."

"What about it scares you?" asked Cory

Suddenly, Ashley trembled. "I wish I knew. I keep hoping I'll wake up one morning and remember my past. Is that possible?"

"Yes. It is more than possible. It's probable."

"Then I don't need hypnosis?"

"It may be a faster route."

"I think I'll wait it out," Ashley said.

"If you change your mind, call me and we'll try again."

"How much do I owe you?" Ashley pulled out her wallet and rummaged for bills. She seemed relieved to pay and avoid further contact with Cory.

Cory calculated her travel time and the sessions. She accepted the cash and pulled out a pad and pen and handed it to Ashley. "Please jot down your post office box number and I'll send you a receipt. Please write your new phone number."

Normally, Cory welcomed therapeutic challenges, but this one was too darn frustrating.

⸗12⸗

Initially relieved after leaving Ashley, Cory felt a wave of disappointment as she approached home. She tried to be objective about her failure with Ashley.

After all, it was a difficult case from the start, and she had thought Ashley's obsession with the furnishings compromised therapy. Now, she reconsidered. On an unconscious level, antiques may be linked to Ashley's past—and to her trauma.

Cory had tried to pursue Ashley's obsession with the antiques, but the young woman wasn't ready to explore in that direction. She seemed fearful of dredging up anything that could be tied to the traumatic event preceding her amnesia.

Cory had ended the session out of frustration. Feeling manipulated, she also didn't trust Ashley's personality swings. Cory had succumbed to a gut reaction and allowed it to disrupt her work.

She reminded herself of what she advised fledgling therapists: "We can't like every patient," and "Trust your gut."

It was Saturday afternoon and she was alone. Usually, she welcomed solitude, but not today. She expected Betty, her best friend and trusted colleague, would return from her European trip this weekend. Give her a few days to acclimate to the time zone and she would be ready to share her refreshing experiences, and listen to Cory's tale of woe. Betty's insight was precious.

When Cory returned home, there was a phone message from Betty. "If you're free for lunch at Humphrey's this Tuesday at noon, please calendar it in. Check with me later. I'll be up late."

She heaved a sigh of relief and called Betty. "I'm suffering from jet lag, Cory, or else I'd ask you over. Place is a mess, anyway."

"Not necessary. First, welcome back. I missed you. I want to hear all about your trip, but I can wait until Tuesday."

"Hey, Cory. Something is wrong. I can tell it from your voice. Give it here."

"You're very perceptive, Betty."

"So are you. Without a mirror, we can't see something behind us that our friend sees."

"For sure, Betty."

"So what's up?"

Sparing no detail, Cory proceeded to tell her about Ashley.

Betty didn't interrupt. "This is a bizarre case. It doesn't seem like the common variety retrograde amnesia. She would have been more willing to try hypnosis, or the newspaper article. One thing for sure, she doesn't appear trusting."

"True. I think she wants to hide something from herself or from me. At times I felt the amnesia could be a put-on. I'm considering a tentative diagnosis of dissociative identity disorder."

"We're on the same page. You don't have enough information to make any diagnosis, nor do you need one at this early stage. You're not billing insurance. You went out of your way to help this woman. That she still claims to have amnesia isn't your fault."

Cory sighed. "Well, if she calls, it'll be interesting.

"Quit berating yourself. We'll talk on Tuesday. Ciao, Cory. Oh, before I go, how's it going with Ben?

"He's in the U.K. and is supposed to return soon, but he's either too busy for me, or has lost interest."

"He's probably swamped with work and there is a time difference."

"Yes, I know, but when he calls, he sounds like he's in a hurry to end the conversation."

"Cheer up and we'll talk on Tuesday. Ciao, Cory."

"*Au revoir, bon amie.*"

⸗13⸗

By the time Tuesday rolled around, Cory had decided to push Ben out of her mind. She realized the futility in trying to figure out the cause of his evasion or disinterest.

Larry arrived early and was waiting in the reception room.

An ideal patient, he participated fully in sessions, and worked hard on his problems. Cory was always eager to see him, but this time was special. He'd have news about his Ashley.

He stepped into the consulting room, sighed, and sank into the chair. "I don't know what to make of it," he said, shaking his head from side to side. I haven't been able to reach Ashley. She seemed genuinely interested. I took your advice and called her several times, but there was no answer. Nothing. *Nada*. No message to the caller. It just rang about a dozen times each time I phoned. Maybe she was just playing with me and had no intention of meeting me. That's why she gave me a wrong number."

"Listen, Larry. I trust your earlier judgment about her. You said you were pleasantly surprised with how well you two got along. I doubt this woman would deliberately give you a wrong number. How would she know that number didn't work? Something may have happened to her or to her phone. Did you give her your number?"

"I don't remember. That was sure dumb of me."

"You were so excited about your good fortune, that nothing else entered your mind. We don't always learn from our mistakes, but this one you'll remember. You may still hear from her. You can find out which gallery in La Jolla is planning an artist reception and attend by yourself."

"Oh, for sure that'd be embarrassing." Larry looked as though Cory had just told him his fly was open.

"If she gave you the wrong number in error, and she attends the reception, she may have realized her error and would be happy to see you again. "

"Do you think so?"

Cory nodded. "Absolutely."

Larry wrinkled his brow. "What if she's there with a date?"

"She'd have some explaining to do."

He paused, as if picturing the scene. "But it'd be embarrassing for me."

"It would be worse for her." Cory smiled.

"What if she's not there?"

"Don't be surprised if you don't see her. I suspect she could be ill, or had to rush out of town for a family emergency, and in her haste left her phone at home. Such stuff happens."

"I never thought of anything like that," Larry said, rubbing his chin.

"We're still working on your tendency to jump to negative conclusions."

Larry nodded. "You're right. I should attend the event anyway, just in case there was a foul up in our communication. I've never been to an artist reception before. I don't know what to expect."

Figuring she'd made some headway, Cory proceeded. "When a gallery hosts a reception, it's a festive event open to the public. Visitors stroll around to examine the artworks and are usually offered refreshments, perhaps a glass of wine and some edibles. Their hands are busy sipping and munching. It's low-key with no pressure to purchase. Sometimes there's music—a guitarist or a trio."

"I'd feel awkward going there alone."

"I've seen people attending solo. It can be a nice way to meet others with a common interest." Cory enjoyed setting the scene for Larry.

The session continued much like others with him: Larry feeling unworthy of attention from women, and Cory's attempts at bolstering his unjustified poor self-image. Although his progress was slow, he had come a long way and Cory would not give up on him.

Much to her delight, at the close of the session, Larry rose from the chair and said, "Okay, I'm ready to brace myself for the reception."

Would there be a secondary gain for Cory? Would she learn if Larry's Ashley was her patient? Both of those young women were artists, and probably Ashley Hogan was either a student or on the art faculty at U.C.S.D.

She decided to contact the university and try to learn if Ashley was enrolled, or on the staff. Online, Cory found the phone number and waited for over a dozen rings with no response. Possibly the economy forced the school to reduce the number of personnel.

A glance at the wall clock reminded her she had to meet Betty for lunch in thirty minutes. She grabbed her purse and headed for her old Beemer.

⸗14⸗

Whenever she was near the ocean, Cory usually experienced a keen sense of calm. It had been her special balm to relieve distress. In the years before dependence on cell phones, the routine drive down Camino del Mar had afforded a panacea, but no longer.

She passed familiar shops and restaurants, and braked at stop signs. Too often she hit the brakes for pedestrians daring to cross in the middle of the street mesmerized by their cell phones. Such devices commanded the users' full attention and were perilous in traffic. Cyclists weaved in and out of the narrow bike lane taken up by delivery trucks. Drivers had to be on the alert.

She had left early enough for the slow drive.

Soon Torrey Pines and the ocean came into view. Cory drove over the old bridge still awaiting repairs after many years. She breathed a sigh of relief, anticipating the rest of her drive would be more pleasant.

She passed the golf course, research, and medical buildings, and from the corner of her eye, she saw university students safely run along the jogging path.

Cory rolled down the car windows and inhaled the scent of tall eucalyptus trees lining the street. She could save ten minutes by driving on the freeway, but she preferred the coastal route.

She arrived at Humphrey's about ten minutes early. Dina showed her to the familiar, secluded booth where Betty sat, engrossed on her mobile phone screen. The plush booth was out of earshot of other diners, making it an ideal place for private conversations. The two confidantes met there regularly.

Janet, a tall, attentive server with an impeccable memory for the dining choices of her regular guests, greeted her. Betty wiggled out of the booth to hug Cory.

"You beat me here, Betty," Cory said.

"My last patient of the day cancelled, so I got through early. Anyway, after vacations, my practice is usually slow, but never like this. All the shrinks in my building are complaining. What's causing this?" Betty shook her head.

"Have you seen the personal coach ads? It's a blossoming field aiming to replace bona fide psychotherapy."

"You're joking," Betty said.

"I wish I were. In sixteen hours, anyone can become a certified life coach and treat an unprotected naïve public. The New York Times recently reported on a twenty-year-old certified life coach with little real-life experience to draw from, who earned much more than highly trained big-city psychologists."

Betty scowled. "Certified? By what august body?"

"Doesn't matter. Unsophisticated people don't check the validity of the certification agency," Cory said.

"It's hard to imagine people are that unaware, and that legitimate therapy is compromised. What a bummer!" Betty said.

"It must be very disappointing for new psychologists after spending all that time, energy and money on an education and training then barely earning enough to pay their bills."

"The only thing good about being older for me is that I made hay while the sun shone." Betty said.

"Me, too. With fewer patients, I have time for the clerical chores Ann used to handle. You know she's in Boston on a post doc research job."

Betty nodded.

Cory continued. "While I miss her company, it's better for both of us. She's on her way up in her career and I don't have the expense of her salary. My kids are practical. They'll be able to make do with less."

"I wish I could say the same about mine," Betty sighed.

Cory was eager to change the subject. "You look like a sophisticated Parisian with your new hairstyle."

"Is it flattering?"

"Very. A short straight bob works well on your auburn hair and green eyes. You always look beautiful and stylish, Betty."

"Your hair is shorter, too, Cory. Your mitzvah, the *Wigs for Kids* project?"

Cory nodded. She flashed on the bizarre shooting outside the massage salon, but decided not to tell Betty. Why worry her?

"At least you inherited one good thing from your Japanese mother."

"I would have preferred to inherit her musical ability," Cory said.

"Well, I'm glad you didn't inherit her character. She should have told your father before they married that she preferred a musical career to a family."

Betty's concern over the importance of good parenting stemmed from her early work at a foster care agency, and likely, the reason she overindulged her children.

"Betty, I know you'll understand. My birth mother did our family a favor. Grandma wanted more kids, but after my Dad was born, she couldn't have any more. I was a blessing to my grandparents." Tender memories of them moistened her eyes. "Now, tell me about your trip. I've got all day."

Betty grinned and dug into her large purse. Out came a hefty envelope containing over two-dozen photos. "This is half my treasure trove."

Cory spread the photos on the table. "You took some great shots. Each one must hold a good memory."

They reminisced about their respective trips abroad until Janet arrived to take their order.

Over lunch, Cory told Betty all she knew and suspected about Ashley. "I don't know if she'll return to therapy on her own, or if I should call her."

"What feels more comfortable to you?" Betty asked.

"I feel responsible to continue, but I could be kidding myself. Maybe I'm just curious."

"Yes, I know you well, dear one. You're a good-hearted detective. You won't be satisfied until you solve the crime—if there is one," Betty mumbled.

"Well, if she has retrograde amnesia, it's likely she had a traumatic experience. It suggests she witnessed a crime. Perhaps someone she loved was tortured or murdered—probably in that house she abandoned and is too terrified to revisit."

"Perhaps, but she may have a dissociative personality. Remember that famous movie *The Three Faces of Eve* in which the character had multiple personalities?" Betty said.

"Sure. I'm considering that as a tentative diagnosis. It could be why she doesn't remember. I'd know more if I had more time with her."

"There you have it, Cory. You want to solve the mystery. Is Ashley dissociating or does she have amnesia? You can't make a proper diagnosis until you've seen her more than twice."

"Right. Hey, I don't want to obsess about Ashley. New subject: Did you meet anyone interesting on your trip?"

"Yes, indeed. I met a charming Italian tourist in the Paris metro. He mistook me for a Parisian—a logical conclusion since I knew my way around the metro. He asked me directions in French with an Italian accent. I answered him in Italian, but my Italian has an American accent. Turns out he speaks English perfectly. He studied law at Oxford and lives in England. We spent most of our time together in romantic Paris and agreed to meet in London the week before I left for home. I tell you, girl. I was in love."

"Was? What's the problem?"

"Just before I left for home, he told me he's married. As you know, this isn't the first time this has happened to me. I should know better by now, don't you think?"

"I think you're a-dyed-in-the wool romantic. On vacation, it's easy to fall for someone and enjoy a brief romantic interlude. You avoid asking too many questions in the beginning of a relationship because you don't want to know the answer, assuming the guy will be truthful. You enjoy the moment. The future is a huge silent question mark."

"You sure know me, don't you, Cory?"

"After all these years, and all your long vacations, the story ending is usually the same. Face it, Betty. The allure of strangers captivates you."

A tear rolled down Betty's cheek. "I don't want to face it, because I feel I cheated his wife."

"You're a rare and compassionate woman, Betty. Women involved with married men rarely, if ever, consider the wife's feelings."

"So, I'm rare, am I?"

"Yes, and wonderfully compassionate."

"That's part of being a good psychologist."

"Yes. You do have all the parts, Betty."

"Flattery will get you a free lunch," Betty said as she picked up the check.

"Okay, I'm keeping track. Next time, it's on me."

"You know how much I love European fashion, but I couldn't afford anything on my trip. The Euro was too high. How about shopping with me? We'll stroll down Prospect Street like a couple of tourists."

"Sure. It'll be fun," Cory replied.

Cory left her car in the hotel parking lot and rode in Betty's red Acura to downtown La Jolla.

Betty parked at a meter and Cory dropped in a few coins.

They strolled down Prospect Street and stopped at a few galleries. One had a sign outside inviting the public to attend a reception for the artist on Saturday evening.

"I wonder if Ashley will be there?," Cory muttered.

"She would if she assumes her artist identity by Saturday," Betty replied.

"It's so strange how multiple personalities work. I've never treated any. I feel out of my league. I should find someone who specializes in that diagnosis," Cory thought aloud.

"I don't know anyone who lists that specialty. It's too rare. The more I think about Ashley, the more I think you must get to know her better. If she returns for therapy, see what she's like the next session and those that come later. She's too difficult to pigeon-hole now."

"I'll phone her at the Inn to see how she's doing."

"You haven't said one word about that man of yours, Cory."

"There's nothing to say. He's somewhere in the U.K., working on a private matter which he isn't at liberty to discuss. He can't be reached and hardly calls me, and when he does, it's brief, like an obligation. He too, is a mystery."

Betty shrugged. "And you both seemed so right for each other."

"Don't give it a past tense, Betty. I'm hoping he'll check in with me soon and I'll confront him."

They poked their heads into a new boutique. "I feel I owe myself something. I didn't buy anything on this trip. Let's go in and browse."

They tried on a few garments and asked each other's opinion. Betty was content with a cashmere sweater the color of her green eyes and Cory approved, but didn't find anything to fit her tall, lean figure, and had no reason to refresh her wardrobe. She preferred to conserve her money.

After shopping a few hours, Betty drove Cory to her car and they parted, each going home to an expected peaceful solitude.

≉15≉

After returning home, Cory brewed chamomile tea and carried the cup into the cubicle she dubbed, "The Office." She switched on the computer to read her email. The newest mail was from Ben. Her heart raced as she retrieved it and read:

> Cory, my love
>
> I know I've been remiss in not contacting you more often and being brief when I do. If it felt like a brush-off, I'm sorry. The critical matter, over which I have no control, continues. I don't know how long it will take to resolve—a few weeks, or perhaps even months. When it is over, I promise to make up for my absence. I miss you more than ever. I want to hold you in my arms so tightly to feel the beat of your heart. Regrettably, that part of my life must wait. Go on with your life, have fun with your friends and know that you are in my thoughts every day and in my dreams every night.
>
> Ciao,
> Ben

Tears rolled down her cheeks. She read his letter several times, hoping to discover a hidden clue between the lines. She felt Ben wrote the truth, but had concealed something to protect her from it.

Did he have a serious illness?

She paced the hallway wondering what she could do to ameliorate her unease. Overwhelmed by frustration over the unknown, she lay down on her bed and sobbed.

Crying was cathartic. After the tears stopped, she answered Ben's email:

> Dearest Ben,
>
> I appreciate your well-meaning email and your concern for my feelings. Please don't try to protect me from a troubling situation. I sense you are in danger and I'm very worried. I'm concerned that you may be seriously injured, or ill. If so,

please don't shut me out. I want to be with you no matter the circumstance. Given all our dangerous adventures, haven't I proven to you that I can handle difficult situations?

I eagerly await your response.
Love, hugs and kisses,
Cory

After responding to him, she felt better.

Her mobile phone rang. She ran to retrieve it, hoping it was Ben.

"Cory, this is... uh... Ashley. I need to see you as soon as possible." Her tone wasn't demanding. It was pleading. She sounded as she did in their initial session. The current caller was Ashley One. The Ashley she saw at the Inn was Ashley Two.

Cory checked her appointment schedule. "I can see you tomorrow morning at ten. You can park in the dedicated space next to my office."

"Thank you. I'll be there promptly," Ashley One replied.

⸗16⸗

Cory checked her trusty Timex at 9:55 A.M. Ashley hadn't made a fuss about coming to the office. Was it because Cory made it clear that it was her expectation, or was the patient in her Ashley One mode when she made the appointment?

Ashley arrived exactly on time wearing a form-fitting black dress with a demure V neckline, black hose, and a pair of mid-heeled black patent leather pumps. As usual, her hair was rolled into a neat bun. Except for a tint of pinkish colored lipstick, her pale face was clear of make-up. She looked the part of a salesperson in a gallery or a high-priced boutique. Ashley seated herself, and crossed her ankles. Her style and demeanor were that of a well-schooled debutante.

"How are you, Ashley?"

"I'm feeling less frightened, although I've had a few troublesome flashbacks."

Cory wanted to discuss their last session, but flashbacks took precedence. "Tell me about them."

"On the surface, they seemed innocent, but still they gave me the creeps. For example, yesterday, while I was alone eating plain waffles at the hotel, suddenly I remembered eating waffles with strawberries in what seemed to be the same setting, but I wasn't alone. I was with uh...a woman. It seemed like she was my mother!"

"Can you describe her or anything else that came up at that moment?"

"It was vague, like a dream. At first it was pleasant, but suddenly, I became frightened. Do you think I could be going mad?"

"No. I don't see any such evidence. You've suffered a trauma. It caused you to lose memory of your past. Naturally, it is bound to be disconcerting."

Through teary eyes, she looked up at Cory. "I'm afraid to find out what happened?"

"That's understandable. You're safe here. We'll handle it together."

"How do we begin?"

"Tell me about the other flashbacks."

Edging closer toward Cory, Ashley placed her elbows on her knees and appeared ready to whisper a secret.

"A man, tall and thin, approached me while I was getting ready for bed. He seemed somewhat familiar, but I didn't have a good feeling about him, as I did with the other flashback I mentioned."

"Tell me more about that feeling."

"He gave me the creeps." Ashley shuddered.

"Of course. An unfamiliar man in your bedroom is frightening."

"I don't know what he was doing there. Most definitely he was menacing."

"Describe him.

Ashley closed her eyes and trembled. "Dark eyes, slick black hair. Oh, it looks like he has a pencil-thin mustache, like some old-time actor."

"This is good, Ashley, you're digging into your memory bank and pulling up the memory of an old-time actor—one that you may have seen in an old movie. Have you watched any old movies after you lost your memory?"

"I want to avoid anything on TV that could scare me. I watch HG-TV for entertainment. As you'd expect, I especially enjoy Antique Roadshow."

"It's encouraging that you remember about scary stuff on TV."

"I do remember lots of things. I remember to brush my teeth and my favorite toothpaste. I remember the name of our President. I remember Del Mar shops and the beach, how to drive, and I know deep inside that I'm a competent person." She paused, brushed an out-of-place hair away from her face and stared down at the floor. "I also remember that I wasn't very polite to you the last time we met. I apologize for my bad manners."

The apology was a revelation. It meant that Cory would dismiss the tentative troublesome diagnosis of dissociative identity disorder.

"Apology accepted. Your frustrating situation probably caused you to be on edge. It's understandable. "I'm confident that your memory will come back."

"How much longer must I wait?"

"I can't predict exactly when, but hopefully soon. Let's work on helping it along. You're safe here, so let's go back to the menacing man. Do you remember anything else about him?"

Again, she closed her eyes. "Yes, he's wearing a tuxedo."

"Good. You remember what a tuxedo looks like. Is it a modern or old-fashioned style?"

"Old-fashioned, I think. Oh, my. I remember dancing with a man in a tuxedo, when I was a little kid! But it's vague. He seemed very tall to me, but I was a little kid."

"Wonderful. As you start to remember, stuff may come back in spurts. Allow yourself to flow with the memory. Capture it. Jot it down."

"I am actually feeling more hopeful. Thank you, Cory."

'You're very welcome. Any other flashbacks?"

"No, but I had a dream. Could that be significant?"

"Yes, please go on."

"I'm driving up the coast. The radio is on and I'm singing. That's all."

"Are you alone?"

Ashley's eyes shut. "It feels like someone is next to me. Someone comforting."

"What are you singing?"

Ashley clasped her hands over her ears to muffle outside sounds that might interfere with her concentration. "I love you Porgy. Yes, I'm singing a duet with the person next to me."

According to Freud, dreams are the royal road to the unconscious, but Cory had too little information about Ashley to understand her dreams and flashbacks.

If Ashley regained fragments of her memory, it may be possible to weave them together in a meaningful way.

Cory had planned to use hypnosis to bring Ashley back to her early memories—perhaps to a safer time in her life, but the material the young woman presented was fruitful. She wanted to take advantage of it while Ashley was on a roll.

"Oh, my, I'm having another flashback. I'm sitting on the lap of a woman with long, silky blonde hair. I can't resist the urge to touch it and feel the softness. As I do, the sun and shadows cast different shades. I marvel at that. She's smiling at me."

"How do you feel?" Cory asked.

"I feel safe and happy, like she's my mother!"

Cory resisted the temptation to shout, "Wow!"

"She's a wonderful mother. Kind, sweet, smart, talented. I wish I knew where she is now and what happened to her. I can only go back to singing in the car."

"You're on a roll, Ashley. In what ways was your mother talented?"

"She had a beautiful voice—in the dream." Ashley rubbed her head and became silent.

Cory waited.

"Suddenly, I have a horrid headache. Too much mental stimulation, you think?"

"It's very emotional bringing up this stuff. Would you rather stop for now?"

"You're the doctor. What's your advice?"

"I'd like to continue to see how far we can go. You can stop anytime you think it's too difficult."

"May I have some water, please?"

Cory reached for the water pitcher, filled a goblet and handed it to Ashley.

Ashley sipped in silence.

"A penny for your thoughts, Ashley."

"That's an odd expression, Cory. Can't remember ever hearing it, but then again, I've lost my memory. Haven't I?"

"You haven't lost your verbal memory. What I said is an old-fashioned expression that you may not have heard before today."

"I'm scared to find out about the man in my dream and where my mother is." Trembling like a leaf in the wind, she hugged herself.

"Do you think they're connected?" Cory asked.

"Yes, yes. They must be," Ashley said.

"What makes you think so?"

"Because they're the only people I can remember from my past."

Cory nodded "In time, others will resurface."

Ashley rubbed her forehead. "I have a terrible headache. Let's stop now. I'll call later for another appointment." She stood and strode to the door.

At the window, Cory watched Ashley stumble to her car at the moment Susan arrived on foot. Susan turned her head and stared at Ashley.

Cory took Susan's early arrival as a sign of readiness to confront her problems. Years ago, many therapists hypothesized that patients who arrived early were anxious, latecomers were hostile, and on-timers were compulsive. It may have been an old joke contrived by anti-therapy people.

Cory usually allowed fifteen minutes between patients to chart progress and add information. In Ashley's chart, she highlighted the notation to follow up on the tuxedo-clad, menacing man and the woman who appeared in both her flashback and dream. She made a note in her schedule to check on Ashley by phone later in the day.

Cory opened the office door for Susan, dressed in running shoes, shorts, and a tee shirt emblazoned with the word SUPERWOMAN. Her hair was braided into a ponytail.

"Pardon my appearance. I'm planning a run after our session. The young lady who stumbled out of your office looked very familiar to me. I greeted her, but she ignored me. It's driving me nuts, trying to figure out from where I know her. What's her name?"

"I'm sorry, Susan, I'm required by law to protect patient confidentiality."

Susan shrugged. "All I want to know is her name, not her business with you."

"I understand, but it is unethical to reveal a patient's identity without a signed consent. If you remember from where you know her, do share it with me. I know it's irritating and I'd like to know that you've solved the mystery." Cory smiled.

"It's not that important. It's not why I'm here."

Susan was a willing patient and open to discuss the cause of her betrayal. The effects were painfully obvious. She knew she had made a dreadful mistake and wanted to learn how to make amends.

To that end, Cory suggested that Susan should consult Tom. Susan feared that he would never trust her again and the damage she caused was irreparable. They were due for a conjoint session in a few days.

≈17≈

When Cory turned on her computer and clicked on her confidential email box, she had a surprising message from Bruce Xavier Smith, Ph.D.

> *Subject:* THREAT
> *Message:* Recently, I received a blackmail letter. Let's discuss a plan to bring the blackmailer to justice. Can we meet somewhere soon?

An intelligent move to demonstrate he was legitimate, Bruce Xavier Smith provided his mobile phone number and website address.

She checked his website and learned his office location was in Orange County, about an hour or two north of San Diego. She figured they could meet face to face somewhere between their respective offices, or discuss a plan over the phone to unmask the blackmailer and seek justice.

His photo and bona fides suggested he was her contemporary and legitimate. She phoned his mobile and left a message asking him to return her call.

She also replied to his email:

> Dear Bruce,
> Thanks for contacting me. If you haven't already done so, for your peace of mind, I suggest you contact your malpractice insurance carrier. If you're still interested in pursuing the blackmailer, we could join forces to plan an entrapment.
> Please let me know.
> Cory

Pleased for the satisfaction and excitement of snaring a blackmailer, Cory smiled as she clicked "send" before signing off her email.

Bruce's email served to take Cory away from obsessing about Ashley's condition. In her spare time, she had read about retrograde amnesia and concluded her diagnosis was correct. While she had earned a certificate proclaiming her mastery in the technique of hypnosis, and had successfully used it in other situations, she had never used it with retrograde amnesia. As a competent practitioner, she questioned her hesitation to use it with Ashley. What was she afraid of dredging up?

Cory preferred not to swim in uncharted waters.

A run on the crowded beach on Sunday morning was impossible. A jog in the neighborhood would have to do. As she was tying her shoes, the phone rang.

"Hi Cory, it's Joe. I know it's a short notice, but we haven't seen you in a long time. We miss you and we're hoping you'll come over today." Roberta picked up the extension. "How are you, old buddy?"

"Fine Ro, I'm glad you called."

"Lucky to find you at home for a change. We can't keep up with your exciting adventures. Have you any time today to visit us?"

"Yes. I'd love to."

"Terrific. I'd appreciate your trustworthy critique of my new dish. I need your approval before it goes into my cookbook."

"When should I come?"

They agreed on lunch at noon. Cory hoped she'd have a chance to discuss Ashley with Joe.

With little time for her regular run, she chose a rarely used path around the golf course. When she was halfway back, she tripped on a stray golf ball. She hobbled home to treat her scraped knee, and vowed to delete that path from her running choices.

After cleansing and dressing the wound, she sponged herself off, donned a red silk shirt and a loose blue denim skirt. She stepped into her sensible loafers.

Lunch was always casual at Joe and Roberta's. She stopped at a market for bottle of Merlot and doggie treats before driving south on the coast to her friends' impressive digs.

On her drive, she thought about their long friendship. She had met Joe in grad school where they had become close friends and colleagues, long before Roberta entered his life. Joe concentrated his efforts in psychoanalytic training and remained in New York while

Cory chose California. They kept in touch. Fast-forward to ten years later when he met and married beautiful, savvy, talented Roberta. At first Roberta perceived Cory as a threat, but when she got to know her, she realized there had never been any romance between Joe and Cory. She accepted Cory as her own friend, too.

Several years ago, Joe and Roberta had relocated from their upscale Manhattan co-op to a La Jolla mansion protected by state-of-the-art security and a pair of German Shepherds named after two famous psychoanalysts: Ziggy, for Sigmund Freud, and Otto, for Otto Rank. Graduates of canine finishing schools, Ziggy and Otto were well-behaved pets and trained watchdogs.

Cory would be forever grateful to her friends. They had provided refuge when her life was in danger from a serial killer over a dozen years ago, when Ziggy and Otto were still pups. They were affectionate and protective of her, too. She regarded them as members of her extended family.

In twelve minutes, she approached the walled estate on a hill surrounded by tall pine trees, a few palms, and an assortment of blooming foliage. The multi-level pink stucco house, sporting a red-tile roof resembled a Mediterranean Villa. Its spectacular setting overlooking the pounding surf was breathtaking. In the evening, one could see whitecaps illuminated by the moon.

Joe and Roberta were her oldest, dearest, and richest friends. The discrepancy between their finances didn't take away from their history and affection for each other. Joe earned a respectable income from his work as a busy psychoanalyst. Roberta, a woman of many talents, was also a shrewd investor. She managed to amass a fortune from their joint earnings. A few of her well-researched financial tips had helped Cory finance Rachel and Noah's educational expenses.

As she approached the wrought iron gate to call in, the gate opened. Ziggy and Otto barked a greeting and ran to her. Well cared for, the dogs didn't seem to age. As she bent down to pet them and offer treats, she winced from the pain in her knee.

"What's wrong, Cory," Joe asked.

"I tripped on a golf ball and scrapped my knee."

Roberta raised her eyebrows and frowned. "You're golfing? "You?"

"Of course not. I was jogging on a path adjacent to the golf course."

"What were you thinking?" Joe rolled his eyes.

"My mind was on a difficult patient."

"You two can discuss it after lunch," Ro said, linking arms with Cory.

They entered the dining room overlooking the Pacific. Cory handed Ro the bottle of wine. The table was set and lunch was already on the plates.

"If I'd been thinking straight, I would have asked if you were serving fish. Then I'd have brought white wine," Cory said.

"This will do nicely," Ro said, uncorking the bottle. "Red is healthier."

After a spectacular, tasty, healthy lunch of quinoa mixed with shredded vegetables and cold salmon, topped with a light lime honey dressing, Cory felt renewed. "Is this the dish you want me to critique?"

Roberta nodded. What's your opinion?"

"Paradise. Heaven. Succulent. Award winner."

"May I quote you on that?"

"Even though I'm not a genuine food critic?"

Ro smiled. "Among your friends, you are."

Cory understood her meaning. Among her friends Cory's reputation as a non-professional food critic was well-known. Plans for dining out were made only after consulting her. When it came to food preparation and presentation, Cory was considered the authority. She figured her friends indulged her because she was the fussiest person they knew. If she liked it, they would, too. She preferred to describe herself as "appropriately discriminating."

"We'll have dessert later," Ro said. Come on into the library where you can fill us in on what's new with you and the kids."

With no children of their own, Roberta and Joe regarded Rachel and Noah as their family, and doted over them. "Friends are often closer than relatives." Grandma used to say, "You can choose your friends, but not your relatives."

For Cory, having no living relatives apart from her father, now an Israeli citizen, and her children, long-time friends were highly valued. It was a comfort to know they could always count on each other.

Cory enjoyed sharing the latest news in her children's lives.

"Rachel's part time job at the community college is going well. She's enthusiastic about the American Government course she's teaching, but it's not enough to live on. However, I'm pleased to say that glowing reports from her students prompted the Chair of the Political Science Department to promise her additional courses next semester. It would qualify her for the usual benefits."

"And her social life?" asked Roberta.

"It's good. She's dating Paul, a young attorney in the D.A.'s office. He's successfully prosecuted a few bad guys."

Joe and Roberta applauded Rachel's success. "And what is Noah up to?" Joe asked.

"Noah remains passionate about nature photography. The good news is he's negotiating a publishing contract."

"That's wonderful. Any romantic interest?" Joe asked.

"Not yet. I think it's because he's shy. He's usually hiding behind a camera."

"And Ben, your exciting retired FBI agent?" Roberta winked.

"He's back in the U.K. on a private matter. I'm worried about him because he doesn't call very often and he may have to stay there for a few months." Cory wrung her hands.

"He seems to be the type who wouldn't want to worry you. Maybe he's on a secret mission," Joe said.

"No. He told me it wasn't government-connected."

"He may have had to provide a cover if it was defense-related," Ro offered.

Cory shrugged. "I miss him and I'm really worried, but there's nothing I can do, but wait."

"Please let us know when you hear from him," Roberta said, rising from her chair.

"Let me distract you, Cory," she continued as she walked to the piano. "I'd like you to hear a piece I composed."

Roberta, a classically trained pianist, began to play in the style of an accomplished jazz pianist.

Watching in amazed delight as Roberta's graceful fingers danced on the keyboard, Cory tapped the rhythm on the arm of the chair.

When Roberta finished, Cory stood and cried, "Bravo, Bravo! Such talent, I'm *kvelling*."

"I thought you'd like it. Maybe we can do a duet: you on percussion, and me on the piano."

"I'm not in your league," Cory admitted.

"Just for fun. We're not auditioning for a gig," Ro said.

"Okay. Next time I'll bring my bongos."

Cory was proud of her multi-talented friend. A superb cook, excellent musician, and an antique historian, Roberta lectured on ancient artifacts and had owned an antique gallery in La Jolla until a few years ago.

Her thoughts turned to Ashley and what the young woman perceived as precious antiques at the Inn.

"How would someone detect an authentic antique from a fraudulent one?" Cory asked.

"It usually requires an expert. I should be able to determine the vintage by the age of the materials and how they were fashioned. Why do you ask?"

"I'm curious. Someone told me about an inn in Cardiff furnished with genuine antiques. I doubt they'd be in the lobby of an inn."

Roberta rolled her eyes.

"Unless someone stored them there for safekeeping, pretending they're copies," Cory said.

"Why would they do that? Unless they were stolen and... Roberta hesitated.

"And stored there until they were safe to sell?" Cory finished the sentence.

The ah-ah moment had occurred followed by silence. Cory didn't know how to follow up without revealing a confidence, which she could do with Joe, her colleague. It was unusual for her to sit quietly. She glanced at Joe.

Joe rose. "Hey, Cory, didn't you want to discuss a case with me?"

"Okay, you shrinks. I've got a lot to do for the next half hour or so. Will that give you enough time before dessert?"

"Thanks, Ro. Cory followed Joe into his office.

She took residence in the smaller of the two armchairs, while Joe squeezed into the larger one.

Since last year, his weight had increased and his hair decreased. The difference from a year's absence was striking. She remembered the time when he was a young, thin, lanky, bushy-haired, bearded grad student. Now, he had matured into a middle-aged, paunchy, balding man. His earlier dark beard now sprinkled with gray. She hadn't paid particular attention to her own age progression, focusing more on physical fitness and nutrition. Some of her patients, like Tom and Susan, did their best to maintain their youthful appearance, probably with the help of cosmetic surgery and exercise.

"I'm in listening mode," Joe said.

She launched into her *shpiel* about Ashley, speaking rapidly to make sure they'd have enough time to make something of the case.

"Slow down, please, Cory. We have time."

"But Ro mentioned a half hour."

"Yes, a half hour or so. She didn't etch the time in concrete and she sensed you want to pick my brain. She'll wait patiently if we're here two hours. She's got a lot of stuff she can do. Wasn't her jazz piece something?"

"You married an amazing woman, Joe. I'm so happy for you. You deserve each other."

Joe smiled. "Only one thing missing. Ziggy and Otto are old dogs and they can't make up for our lack of children, but we can chat about that another time."

Cory sensed his pain. He would have made a terrific father.

"Please continue, Cory."

She took a deep breath before reciting details of her few sessions with Ashley.

Joe stroked his beard, a typical habit of male analysts.

"So far from what you've seen of her, dissociative identity disorder does not seem to fit. I agree with your diagnosis. You understand that retrograde amnesia can clear up by itself, but it's better for the patient to have supportive therapy, especially since she appears to be entirely on her own. I think you're proceeding well, by letting her lead the way and you showing her you're there for her. She may not be ready for hypnosis. She's still scared to confront the trauma. I think you're right in playing it safe."

"The sleuth in me is tempted to find out if the antiques are genuine."

"Despite your adventures into the realm of real detective work, it is not your profession. We love you and want you with us for a long time. And Rachel and Noah need you too. Please don't play the *shtarker*."

"Are many of your patients Yiddish speaking, Joe?"

"You're digressing from my request."

"Don't worry. I hope I've learned from my mistakes. I realize I'm not invincible."

"Seems to me, I've heard that song before, Cory," Joe sang.

"I appreciate your concern. And for a moment, let's talk about you. You're a great analyst for others, but not for yourself. You're too sedentary and need to exercise on that state-of-the-art equipment you bought for the unused room you've dedicated as 'The Gym.'

"Okay. Tit-for tat. I promise to use the gym if you promise not to poke your nose into dangerous places."

"It's a deal, Joe." She paused. "I have an idea. Since Roberta is an expert in antiquities, if you visited the Inn as prospective guests, she could eye the furnishings and let me know if they're genuine."

"Three concerns, Cory. One, it's not exactly kosher to pretend to be prospective guests. Two, Roberta may have a trained eye, but she may need more sophisticated tools to determine if the items are genuine. Three, assuming she could tell a genuine antique from a copy without using sophisticated tools, how would you use the information?"

"I'm curious about Ashley's obsession with the furnishings—her insistence that they're genuine, her comfort in that spooky environment. This suggests an uncanny familiarity that may be a clue to her trauma-induced amnesia."

Joe paused and inhaled deeply. "You may be on to something. I'll think of a way to interest Ro without tying it to your case, but remember my friend, curiosity killed the cat."

"Thanks, pal." She stood, and opened her arms to give Joe a hug.

Strolling into the dining room, they inhaled the scent of cinnamon and vanilla. Roberta had opened the oven door and was ready to remove the dessert. "Just in time. You found me just in time," she sang.

After the tasty treat, Cory embraced her friends. She promised to keep in touch more regularly and would report an update on Ben.

⸗18⸗

Before starting her car, Cory's concern over Ashley's headache deepened. She phoned the Inn to speak with her. The clerk rang her room, but there was no response. "Have you seen Ashley today?" Cory asked.

"No. I'd have noticed her. It's very quiet here. We have a skeleton staff and very few guests."

"I'd appreciate it if you'd send someone to her room to check on her. Please tell her Cory wants to talk with her."

"Of course. The staff knows about her condition. Olivia, our maid is quite compassionate. She's right here. She'll check the room. Hold on, please."

"Thank you, Cory said.

She heard the clerk repeat her request in Spanish.

"*Si, voy ahora.*" the maid replied.

The clerk resumed her conversation with Cory. "It's usually half full this time of year, but we didn't expect it to be this slow. Must be a sign of a bad economy, don't you think?"

"Probably. The place has a great location and the interior decorator made it resemble a museum."

"Yes. She's an incredible decorator, for sure. She changes our style every few years. Last time it was contemporary. Too much stainless steel. Some guests were put off by the coldness. One guest said it reminded him of a science lab. Another time she filled us with funky stuff. Did she really think our guests want to live in a college dorm? It didn't go off well even though we're near Swami's, the most popular surfing beach around here."

"It must be very expensive to change the design so often," said Cory.

"Oh, we don't buy the furnishings. We rent them. The owners told me it's a very good deal."

Cory knew nothing about the management of bed-and-breakfast places, but she considered the furniture rental arrangement worthy of inquiry.

Was the rental company tied to a robbery scheme? Antiques could yield high sums and were probably insured against theft. Was it possible to conduct such a heist and store highly valuable furnishings inside unwitting hotels and inns? Wasn't there a potential danger that a sophisticated guest would recognize important objects and link it to a robbery? Even if the possibility were remote, would it be worth the chance?

She wanted to learn more. "A real estate agent I know would love such a deal. The rental of fine furnishings would help market her empty properties. May she contact you for a referral to the decorator?" asked Cory.

'Hold on a moment; here comes Olivia."

A muffled conversation between the clerk and the maid ensued before the clerk spoke to Cory.

"Ashley's is not in her room and her luggage is packed. Olivia looked for her, but she's nowhere on the premises. Olivia checked the parking lot. Ashley's car is gone, too. Can you imagine that? After how well we accommodated her, and she didn't even have the decency to tell us she was checking out."

"Let's not jump to a conclusion. Maybe she was tired of staying in her room and decided to go for a drive," Cory said.

"But why would she pack her luggage?" the clerk asked.

"Perhaps she planned to use the luggage to carry her clothes to the cleaners. Or she was lonely and wanted to check out other places. After all, she's a single woman on her own," Cory said without conviction.

"Well, yes. She doesn't strike me as the type who'd run off without paying," the clerk said.

"Since she didn't take her luggage, it suggests she plans to return. She told me she is very comfortable at the Inn. When you see her, please tell her I phoned and left a message for her to call me."

* * *

As Cory approached home, she noticed the absence of Real Estate Rita's luxurious Lexus van from the usual place in the driveway. She hoped Rita was out showing property to an eager client. Cory's anticipated discussion about the rental furnishings at the Inn would have to be postponed.

Cory found it amusing that a few neighbors confused her with glamorous Rita simply because both were middle-aged, tall, lean, and had thick black hair.

Dolled up in expensive garb and perfectly applied makeup, Rita was very attractive and had the sophisticated appearance probably expected of a realtor for the rich—a sharp contrast to plain-faced Cory in comfy duds.

The two women had little in common apart from enjoying an occasional jog on the beach together.

Despite the differences in their style and work, they were good neighbors, alerting each other on the rare occasion of a community problem. They kept each other's phone and mobile numbers and security code in the event of an emergency.

In years past, when Rita sold an expensive property, she would invite Cory to a lavish celebration with her real estate colleagues. With the lull in sales, such invitations had ceased.

After locking the door behind her, Cory kicked off her shoes and curled up in her favorite chair with the Sunday New York Times. She clicked on the stereo tuned to jazz FM 88.3. For a change, they featured oldies from the 30's and 40's. "The Very Thought of You," sung by Billie Holiday drew her attention away from the newspaper and onto thoughts of Ben. Although she enjoyed solitude, she longed to hear from him, if only to assure her he was safe.

Later that evening, the phone rang. Cory hurried to answer, hoping it was Ben.

"It's Ashley. I'd like to see you. I've something important to tell you. "

Cory noted an excitement in Ashley's voice. "I'm free at one o'clock on Wednesday, but you can tell me now."

"I don't want to bother you now. It's about my productive visit to an antique dealer in Laguna Beach. It shows my memory is returning."

"That's terrific! I'm looking forward to hearing about it," Cory beamed.

⸗19⸗

As Cory started out the front door for a neighborhood walk, she noticed an untidy pile of newspapers in front of Rita's front door. Rita was an ideal neighbor—quiet, neat and tidy. It was not her custom to leave her newspapers out for two days.

Her Lexus van wasn't parked in the driveway. Whenever she planned to be away from home overnight, she would ask Cory to check the house and feed her cat, Kitty.

That she had not done any of those things signaled trouble. Rita could be ill, unconscious, or worse. She rang Rita's bell and heard it chime deep inside the house. She waited a few seconds and then pounded on the door to no avail.

Cory dashed home, grabbed Rita's spare key, and hurried back to Rita's house. She unlocked the door, turned off the security alarm, and dropped the newspapers on the hall floor.

Kitty ran to her, meowing. Cory picked her up and stroked her. Kitty purred in response.

Cory called out Rita's name. No response. She checked the garage. The Lexus was there, the engine cold, the trunk empty. Cory searched inside the house, every room and closet. Nothing appeared amiss, but the occupant was gone.

Cory replenished Kitty's empty water and food bowls. She played with the gentle cat while phoning Rita's mobile from the kitchen. There was no answer.

Rita's office phone number was embossed on the memo pad on the kitchen counter. She punched in the number.

"Hi, I'm Rita's neighbor, Cory Cohen. I'm calling from her house. I'm concerned because I haven't seen her for a couple of days. She always alerts me when she plans to be away for a few days, but she hadn't done so. Do you know where she is?

"We're worried about her, too. Rita is reliable. She was supposed to attend a meeting yesterday, but she didn't show up. We called her home and cell phone, but there was no answer."

"Uh-oh. I'd better call the sheriff," Cory said, before disconnecting.

She called 911, identified herself and asked to report a missing person.

"How long has she been gone?" the dispatcher asked.

"At least forty-eight hours. She hasn't picked up her newspapers for two days. As her next-door neighbor, I have her house key. I searched her house and her car. I even looked inside the trunk. No sign of her.

I called her office and was told that it was out-of-character for Rita to fail to show up for a meeting yesterday."

"Please wait by the house. We'll send someone to take your report."

Cory hurried into Rita's house and grabbed a few of her calling cards that she'd seen on the kitchen counter. Rita's photo was on the card. She locked the door behind her.

Cory marched back and forth on the pavement—a proper exercise to reduce her anxiety about her missing neighbor.

About fifteen minutes later, the sheriff's vehicle arrived and a young woman officer hopped out. Tall and trim, she had a rosy complexion, and closely cropped brown hair. She wore wrap-around sunglasses.

"I'm Deputy Annie Lowe," she announced, pulling out a leather-bound notebook and a pen.

"Thanks for coming here so quickly. I'm Cory Cohen, Rita Rivers' neighbor. She handed the deputy a batch of Rita's cards containing her photo.

"It's a good likeness," Cory said.

The deputy took the cards. "Do you know if she has any enemies?"

"Frankly, Rita is a private person. I know very little about her personal life, apart from the fact that she's an excellent neighbor—quiet, clean and neat, and generous. It's well known that she's an award-winning real estate agent, and that she sponsors a local annual run on behalf of mentally challenged children."

When asked for a more complete physical description, Cory realized that someone—perhaps the shooter—the person who had pursued her on the day of her hair donation, could have mistaken

Rita for her. She shared her concern with the officer. The young officer didn't look up from her notebook as she wrote.

Cory added that she had not been notified of anyone in custody for the shooting outside the massage salon, or any outcome from that incident.

"Do you have a suspect?" Deputy Lowe asked, looking up at Cory.

Cory shook her head, "No."

"I have sufficient information to look into that matter for you. I promise to follow up and let you know my findings."

"Thank you," Cory said.

"I'll file this missing person report and we'll be on the lookout for her."

"I appreciate your efficiency," Cory said.

Deputy Lowe smiled and returned to the vehicle.

≈20≈

Bruce Smith, the psychologist who had first contacted Cory regarding the blackmailer, emailed Cory again. This time he provided his personal phone number and asked her to phone him at nine that evening.

When she called, he picked up immediately.

Although satisfied with his attorney, Bruce wanted to entrap the blackmailer in order to send a clear message to other potential blackmailers.

He planned to be in Carlsbad directing a continuing education course over the weekend at a resort hotel. The course was scheduled to end at five. Cory agreed to meet him in the hotel lobby on Saturday afternoon at five-fifteen. They would recognize each other from their respective website photos and his continuing education badge.

Excited over formulating a plan to catch a blackmailer, Cory was eager to meet her colleague. She usually found it refreshing to chat with other psychologists.

* * *

At the appointed time, Cory arrived at the resort hotel, expecting to find the lobby abuzz with mental health professionals, but no one was there apart from hotel personnel.

She strolled over to the lobby check-in counter and addressed the clerk. "I'm supposed to meet someone attending the continuing education program here. Do I have the right day?"

"For mental health?" he asked.

"Yes," she said.

"Let me check the program. One moment, please."

The clerk shuffled some papers and looked up at Cory. "The program is probably running over. It was supposed to end at five. You're welcome to wait in the lobby or at the bar."

"Thank you," she said. Spying a comfortable looking armchair facing the elevator, she seated herself upon it to be immediately visible as Bruce exited. She checked her old, dependable Timex watch. It was five-thirty. She figured it must be an exceptionally good conference. Perhaps she should have registered for it. Usually people dash out a few minutes before a conference ends to avoid waiting on a long line to collect their certificates of attendance.

After waiting forty minutes, Cory watched the large elevator door slide open. Over a dozen people, mostly women and three men, all carrying notebooks and wearing nametags on their lapels poured out and rushed past her.

Times have changed, Cory thought. Recently she had read that many more women than men earned advanced degrees compared to twenty years ago.

It was easy to spot Bruce Smith. His photo didn't do him justice. A strikingly handsome, tall, lean man of indeterminate age— anywhere from late thirties to fifty, he had sandy color hair and blue eyes. Wearing a dazzling toothpaste ad smile, he approached her. "Cory?" he asked.

She smiled back and nodded. "I'm thinking the conference was exceptionally good."

"Yes. We ran over schedule because lots of people asked lots of questions. Kurt and I were the presenters, but let's save that for another time. How about a drink at a quiet table in the bar?" He held his hand out to help her out of the chair.

"Thank you, Bruce."

They entered the surprisingly quiet bar and chose a table facing a vibrant multi-flowered garden overlooking a waterfall and a pair of palm trees.

Bruce strolled to the counter and returned with two chilled glasses of white wine. A waiter followed, carrying a platter of tropical fruit and small wedges of assorted cheese. He placed two small forks and cloth napkins on the table. "Complimentary from the kitchen," he said.

Simultaneously, Bruce and Cory thanked him.

"Surprisingly few guests here this weekend," Bruce said. "Do you like living and working in this area?"

She nodded and they continued making small talk to break the ice, until Cory said, "Although I disposed of the blackmail matter with the attorneys, it's hard for me to dismiss it in favor of simple damage control. I'd prefer justice to prevail."

Bruce nodded. "Exactly how I feel. I'm really very pleased to meet you. We're birds of a feather."

Cory picked up some negative undertow from Bruce and instinctively said, "But sometimes a bird in the flock flies in the wrong direction."

"Rarely," Bruce replied. "Don't get cold feet."

Cory thought that if her feet were cold, she'd like someone who looked like him to warm them, but she wouldn't dare say it. She wasn't there for romance. She had a different mission.

"So Bruce, tell me your ideas for snaring the blackmailer?"

"I have only one idea, Cory, and it won't pose a risk. Then, I'd like to hear your ideas."

"Right now, I only have one. I'm ready to listen to yours." She leaned forward.

"Okay. I would send her an invitation to visit me for a frank discussion about her reasons for thinking I harmed her. I'd offer to pay for her damages because I aim for satisfied clients and also because I want to avoid the unpleasantness of a court procedure.

I'd attempt to impress upon her that going that route would not assure the winning of her case, but if we met privately, she would have the chance of at least getting some money—a sum less than $5,000, and she would avoid expensive legal fees."

"You think she'd respond to that?" Cory asked.

"It makes sense to me," Bruce said.

"Bruce, we're dealing with a blackmailer—one who knows the business side of health care. She would be suspicious of you because she knows you don't know her."

His grin chilled her.

"Or do you?"

"As director of the clinic, I supervise a whole lot of psychology interns. One of them may have met with her," Bruce admitted.

"Don't you keep records?"

He grinned. "As I said, I'm very busy."

"Surely you must keep a calendar."

Bruce chuckled. "I used to keep a paper one in the last century, before the advent of smart phones. I would nail a calendar on the inside of a closet door and tear off each page at the end of the month."

"Don't you have an appointment book, Bruce?"

"Got rid of it when I got my iPhone. Now, I record my daily appointments on my mobile. I delete at the end of each day."

"How about lists of charges and payments, tax records, insurance stuff?" Cory asked.

"Thank heaven, I don't need to take insurance. My patients are aware that psychotherapy is too personal for the eyes of insurance personnel and they are rightly afraid of confidentiality breaches. Cash payments insure their confidentiality. I provide receipts to my patients for tax purposes," Bruce explained.

"What about progress notes, records of diagnosis and therapy goals? They may come in handy if there is a break in therapy sessions or the patient terminates for a few years and then returns." Cory said.

"I know it's wrong, but I'm involved with too many things, and frankly, I don't remember how to do this. I'm so busy that paperwork hasn't been a priority."

Cory shook her head, thinking they were not birds of a feather, after all. "If you like, I'll fax you a copy of one of my case summaries. I'll delete sensitive info to protect confidence, but it should be enough to get you started on the right path."

"Mighty kind of you, Cory. I will be most appreciative. Any other advice you may think of will also be very welcome," Bruce said, handing her his business card. "My fax number is on it."

Placing the card in her purse, Cory asked," Do you have a bookkeeper?"

"I use a billing service."

"Bruce, I loathe clerical tasks, too. For that reason, I hired a trustworthy grad student to work for me. She made my professional life so much easier."

Bruce nodded. "I know you're absolutely right, Cory. I should do better, and I have no decent excuse."

Cory shook her head. "This business with Carole Roy is your wake-up call."

"Carole Roy? Who is she?" Bruce asked.

"Probably the fictitious name of my blackmailer."

"Mine is Marion Blake," Bruce said.

"Is the name even slightly familiar to you?" Cory asked

"As I said I have a huge practice and I supervise a large pool of psychology interns. As you know, interns must practice under the name of the supervisor or clinic. All my interns see a lot of people for a several sessions. I don't keep track of the names of the patients we discuss in the numerous supervision sessions I conduct every week. My interns report those sessions as invaluable. I give them my all," he said.

Cory fought the urge to roll her eyes. "Well that is all well and good, but…" she began.

Bruce interrupted, determined to make the point that he was an excellent supervisor. "After they complete their required hours of supervision, they leave and a new batch of interns replaces them. There is a waiting list of trainees who want my supervision enough to wait for an opening. I must be doing something right."

Cory frowned and shook her head. "It's admirable that you're a fine supervisor and your interns learn your therapeutic skills, but it's also important for them and for you to learn how to keep required records related to the work."

Bruce's face reddened. "You are absolutely correct and I should bow my head in shame."

"If we took a national survey, Bruce, I bet recordkeeping is one of our profession's least favorite activities, but it's essential for business survival.

"Maybe like Carol Roy, Marion never came to your office. Have you asked the people you supervise if anyone of them has seen her as a client? She may well be the same person who is trying to blackmail me."

"I asked the current group of interns, but her name was unfamiliar to them. They don't keep records of their former clients. The interns are temporary—they leave after they meet their supervisory hours; then they're off to wherever they can find a job at some agency, usually in their home state."

Amazed by Bruce's nonchalance, his disregard for professional work ethics, Cory shook her head.

"Isn't it your responsibility to keep such records?"

"What? You think I run a sloppy practice?"

"As a supervisor of interns, this is part of your responsibility. You're placing yourself in a dangerous situation," she said.

Bruce frowned. "I realize I should do better with my recordkeeping. You're right about this. It is my wake-up call. Now that you've alerted me, I will concentrate on better business practices.

Next time I'm in your neighborhood, I'd like to take you to a well-deserved dinner."

"Thank you. Perhaps we'll celebrate the capture of the black-mailer."

"Now, Cory, tell me how you would you deal with the black-mailer?"

"Initially, I thought I'd try to trap her by responding to her certified letter with a letter to her post office box. In my letter, I'd start off somewhat like yours. Deny any wrongdoing, but offer to pay off the money to avoid the unpleasantness of going to court. If she agreed, I'd offer to send a thousand dollar money order to reach her on the first of each month.

"I'd mention that if we went to court, she'd probably lose since she has no legitimate proof of any professional visit to me."

"Sounds good to me, but how would you snare her?"

"Easy. I had one scenario, but as we were talking, I considered something else. At first I had considered hiring a private detective to wait at the postal station and watch for the blackmailer to open the box. The detective would snap her photo and follow her. See where she lives, where she goes, but this may be too hard to implement, if the postal station has few patrons.

"Anyway, now that we've tossed this around, I don't think I'll need to spring for the hefty expense of a private eye.

"I just remembered that some time ago, I'd read that using the United States Postal Service for the purpose of blackmail constitutes a federal offense. So, I'll call the postal inspector on Monday and let you know the outcome. Hopefully they can pick her up without my presence since I doubt I could identify her anyway."

"Good idea. Hey, wait a minute," Bruce said. "It occurs to me that the blackmailers could be men. Carole and Marion are old-fashioned masculine names."

"Ah-hah! That's true, and their last names are often first names of men. Roy and Blake. There's an excellent chance that we're targeted by the same blackmailer," Cory noted. In recent years, I've treated more men than women. How about you, Bruce?"

He cupped his chin and seemed to drift off. "I'm counting. Maybe half and half."

"It would be interesting to know if there is anything to the sexually ambiguous names. Maybe the blackmailer deliberately wanted to make identification more difficult.

"It's also tricky in terms of age identification. We'd expect Carole and Marion to be older people and those with the names Olivia and Emily would probably be members of the younger generation. But this is pure conjecture, Bruce."

"Yes. It is puzzling." He grinned. "You sure are a smart, spunky woman! If the postal service goes after her, or him, it should scare the living daylights out of that cheat, and rightfully so. A blackmailer should be convicted and imprisoned. A lesson to regret the scam. I bet no one messes with you."

"I've learned to be wary and alert from personal experience, Bruce. I earned my black belt fairly."

"For real? You're a karate expert?" he asked.

"Correct," Cory said.

Bruce smiled, revealing perfect teeth. "Impressive. Admirable."

"Well, Bruce, I think we both got something out of this meeting. Let's keep in touch." Cory stood, ready for a handshake.

Instead Bruce hugged her. "I'm glad we met. You've been most instructive. Anytime you're in my neighborhood, let me know and we'll have lunch."

"Thank you, Bruce." She doubted he'd have the time for meeting a colleague aware of his poor business habits, but he did seem genuinely grateful for her help.

"And if you hire a record-keeper, I recommend you carefully check references. If you employ an accountant or math major— that'd be great. Usually, we expect them to be punctilious and to love details!"

Bruce nodded. "Let's keep in touch."

She forgot to ask him about his continuing education course. It certainly had nothing to do with record keeping. Either he hadn't learned, or chose not to follow the rules in the business side of practice.

* * *

Almost a week had passed without any news of Rita's disappearance. No mention on radio, TV, Internet, or any newspaper.

Cory had expected to read a notice of Rita's disappearance posted with her photo in the usual places, and was surprised and disappointed at the absence.

It was time to call the sheriff again. The deputy's card was pinned on her kitchen bulletin board, but first she'd attend to Kitty.

After collecting the newspapers from outside Rita's front door and replenishing Kitty's food and water bowls, Cory sat on the couch and waited for Kitty to eat; but Kitty had another idea. She leaped on Cory's lap, expecting to be stroked. Cory obliged and Kitty purred her gratitude.

Cory considered taking Kitty to live with her until Rita's return, but realized cats preferred their own turf. If Rita didn't return soon, Kitty would be Cory's guest. Until then, Cory would visit Kitty at least twice a day.

Rita, as sponsor of an annual charity for mentally challenged children, had always led a well-attended run, publicized in the local newspapers with her name and photo on it. The annual event always took place on July 4th at seven in the morning. The date was approaching in a few weeks. The event was already posted on bulletin boards at local marketplaces.

Although Rita and Cory were good neighbors, they never shared confidences, only the basics about each other. Perhaps a clue could be found from her mail.

Rita's mailbox key hung on a hook in the kitchen. Cory snagged it.

Before opening Rita's mailbox, she unlocked her own box and removed the contents. A preliminary glance showed mostly ads.

A huge pile of mail lay stuffed in Rita's mailbox.

Cory sat on Rita's couch going through the mail, hoping it would yield a clue to her mysterious disappearance. Nothing of a personal nature popped up. No suspicious material to give to the deputy.

Stashed in-between all the ads and flyers in Cory's mail was a purple envelope handwritten in gold lettering. It was from Bruce.

Xavier Smith, Ph.D. It looked like an invitation or a thank you note. She tore it open and read a handwritten personal note:

> Dear Cory,
> I am forever grateful to you for showing me the error of my ways. I hereby promise to never return to those hectic,

sloppy days. You will be pleased to know that I now have a wonderful office manager. I inherited her from my former analyst upon his recent retirement. She promises to keep me on the straight and narrow.

She made copies of your progress notes and case summary outlines. My interns are now required to use them, as I most certainly will—thanks to you!

I decided to ignore the blackmailer and let my malpractice insurance attorney handle it. Please let me know how that matter works out for you. The only good thing that has come of it is meeting you, a wonderful woman, willing to share her knowledge to steer my practice in the right direction.

I hope you will enjoy my small show of appreciation by using the enclosed gift certificates with pleasure. I can personally vouch for the pampering services: massage, facial, pedicure, manicure, in a magnificent setting, complete with the delectable healthy lunch. Kurt and I are regulars there. It's a great place to relax and replenish body, mind, and spirit.

Sincerely,
Bruce

Inside the envelope was a smaller envelope bearing the name *Palliative*. She had heard it was a world famous spa. Cory opened the envelope and pulled out two certificates entitling her to all of the inclusive services and lunch. The certificates could be used for two visits for herself, or for one visit with a friend. She would prefer to invite Betty who would also enjoy the pampering and the time together in a magnificent setting.

Cory left Rita's mail on the couch and went home to collect an appropriate card from her desk drawer to reply to Bruce. She selected one printed with a Matisse painting that she hoped suited his style.

Cory wrote:

> Dear Bruce,
>
> I'm delighted that my comments regarding good business practices and my outlines made a significant impression on you. I'm confident you will be well-rewarded with peace of mind.
>
> Your gift is very thoughtful and generous; I'm touched by your unexpected and magnanimous show of appreciation.
>
> I eagerly look forward to using your wonderful gift.
>
> Re: Blackmail threat. I have decided to do just as you have done—leave it to the malpractice insurance attorneys—they are the experts. We have paid for their services for many years and haven't needed it until now.
>
> Wishing you continued success,
>
> Cory

After sealing and stamping the note to Bruce, she dropped it in the outgoing mailbox and returned to Rita's house.

Seated on her missing neighbor's couch, Cory felt like an intruder. With sadness, she recalled the times when Rita was in the kitchen making coffee for their rare neighborly get together.

She shivered as she wondered about Rita's unexpected disappearance and current whereabouts.

Cory had expected some mention of Rita in the media, but apparently, a local missing woman wasn't important news, even if she was a celebrity among the real estate community and her tiny neighborhood.

If Rita had been injured, or worse, Cory, as the one who reported her disappearance, should have been informed. Perhaps in summer, the sheriff was exceptionally busy responding to problems associated with an increase of tourists, and rowdy racetrack visitors.

But this was a serious matter worthy of attention.

Cory phoned Deputy Lowe. The woman answered the call and said she had provided all the information to Missing Persons and it was no longer her case. She gave Cory another number to call.

Cory jotted the number, and asked if there was any news of her shooter. Deputy Lowe told her it was an open case.

Cory called the number the deputy provided. Placed on hold for an inordinate time, she figured her call was futile and decided to disconnect rather than waste more time before her one o'clock appointment with Ashley.

Her mobile rang. She hoped it was Ben, or law enforcement, but it was Susan, her latest patient.

"I racked my brain and finally remembered the woman stumbling out of your office. She had given an exceptionally fine art lecture and a painting demonstration at the library. Quite memorable."

"Thanks for telling me. I know how annoying it is when you don't remember someone who looks familiar," Cory said.

"I also called for another reason."

"Oh?" Cory asked.

"I want to thank you for helping me get back on track. Tom and I are doing so much better, now. We're going away on an extended trip. We'll call you if we need you when we return."

"You've made a remarkably rapid recovery from the crisis, Susan. I wish you well," Cory said with uncertainty.

Experience taught her that it is unusual for couples to get over such a difficult hurdle so fast. She figured Tom took responsibility for Susan's infidelity and had opted for pharmaceutical intervention.

Cory enjoyed eating a quiet, peaceful lunch alone at home. She whipped a banana into zero-fat, Greek style plain yogurts and tossed in a few organic blueberries. Yummy. Quick. Nutritious. She considered herself a master of healthy fast food.

She drove to the office and parked in her usual space. With a few minutes to spare, she checked the computer for email.

A message with an attachment from Scott Drew, Ph.D., a Beverly Hills colleague, stated he had received a blackmail threat from someone named Lee Thomas claiming to be his patient. The attachment was worded exactly as Bruce and Cory had received. It appeared certain to her that someone was targeting psychologists practicing in southern California's expensive areas.

Again, the mysterious blackmailer used an ambiguous gender first name and a family name that could serve as a masculine first name.

Since the name "Cory" is usually that of a male, was the blackmailer targeting male psychologists exclusively?

Was the blackmailer's motivation purely monetary, or had it sprung from vengeance designed to frighten or intimidate male psychologists?

Could the blackmailer have met a psychologist in another setting in which he or she felt rejected?

Pure conjecture led nowhere. With insufficient evidence, she'd store it in her unsolved blackmail cases file—a total of three. She clicked the reply button and shared what she could with her colleague.

* * *

Ashley arrived promptly at one o'clock. Dressed in tailored blue jeans, a pink silk shirt and black low-heeled shoes, she appeared well-rested and neatly put together.

"I have a suggestion for you Ashley. You may have been, or are a student at U.C.S.D. Perhaps if you drove around the campus, it would spark your memory. You could find out if you were enrolled there. Pop into the local library. Maybe the librarian will recognize you and shed some light."

"Good ideas. I will. I'd like you to know for the first time since I came to see you, I slept well and I wasn't plagued by nightmares."

"That's a good sign. You seem hopeful." Cory wanted to hear details about the nightmares, but Ashley had another agenda.

"Well, as you know I had to get away from the house where all this started. The hotel was a good choice. I feel very comfortable there. The furnishings seemed familiar and the neighborhood seemed to beckon me. Your encouragement that my memory would return has helped, too."

"You mentioned on the phone last night that some memories have surfaced."

"A little more than when we last spoke. I did some research. There's an antique and art dealer in Laguna Beach. His name and location seemed very familiar to me. I called him and made an appointment for yesterday afternoon.

Oddly, I knew exactly where I was going and how to get there. When I arrived, he wasn't there, but his assistant was. I was very disappointed because I had hoped the man and I would recognize each other. I explained my amnesia to the assistant and asked him if he knew anything about me or my family, but he didn't have a clue."

Cory nodded. "And?"

"Well, I told him about the Inn and what I thought were its treasures. He explained that they probably were quality reproductions. He showed me what to look for to determine the authenticity of the furnishings. As he explained it to me, I realized that somewhere, somehow, I already had the information. The memory of it had come back to me. I was very grateful to the man and invited him to have lunch with me at the Ritz Carlton not far from his shop."

"That was generous of you."

"It was the proper thing to do," Ashley replied. "However, he couldn't leave the shop unattended.

"Did you pass the hotel on your way up, or did you remember it?" Cory asked.

"I remembered exactly where it was and how lovely and sparkling everything was, especially dining on the terrace. I remember sitting there with... Oh, it's all so vague." Ashley's eyes closed.

Cory considered this an ideal time for hypnosis. "Take a deep breath and let it out slowly, Ashley."

The young woman complied. Within a few moments, she was ready to go deeper. Cory asked her to describe the scene on the hotel terrace.

"I'm especially happy to be here. It's a wonderful glorious, beautiful day. Clear blue sky. The sun is shining. The weather is warm, not hot. Everything is absolutely perfect in every way. The table is tastefully set. The crystal water goblets shine in the sun. I sip some water. Cooled to perfection. Our waiter is friendly, not overbearing. I admire the fine furnishings and taste the wonderfully prepared food."

Ashley seemed to enjoy her trip back on memory lane to that special tranquil day. Her usual anguished facial expression evaporated.

Her sharp attention to small details was in keeping with her artistic ability.

"Describe your lunch companion," Cory said softly.

Ashley squinted, as though trying hard to focus on an image. "Yes. I'm not alone. I feel that someone is seated with me, but it's a blur. Warped, like a creased photo. I can't make out who it is."

Suddenly, she moaned and began to tremble. Beads of perspiration peppered her brow. "Who the devil are you?" Ashley screeched.

Cory had to act quickly. Continuing hypnosis would possibly yield important information, but it would be at the expense of what she perceived as Ashley's fragile emotional condition noted by the pained expression and moist forehead.

Cory chose to bring Ashley out of the hypnotic state. She would try again later if Ashley's memory didn't surface in due time.

"I feel like I was dreaming. I don't remember what went on. Please tell me," Ashley asked in a soft, little girl voice.

"You described a delightful lunch on the terrace of the Ritz Carlton."

⸗21⸗

Larry arrived early for his session. It was apparent that he had recently visited a barber and a haberdasher. His hair and beard were neatly trimmed and he had replaced his usual outfit of jeans and tee shirt with a pair of pressed khaki slacks and a blue and white stripped button-down shirt. Best of all, the grin on his face predicted his announcement of good news.

"You look wonderful, Larry. Something good must be going on."

"Well, yes. I followed your suggestion and off I went to the gallery reception. It was just as you described. I enjoyed myself a ton. I've never, ever had such a good time!"

"I'm pleased to hear it. Tell me more."

"Well, I met some people from Brazil—friends of the artist. Three guys and two women. They were real friendly to me. After the reception, they invited me to join them at a Brazilian restaurant. It was so much fun. We plan to meet next week at a Latin jam session. One of the guys I met plays guitar."

"That's terrific. It sounds very enjoyable. By the way, you haven't mentioned Ashley."

"Oh, I almost forgot the reason I went to the reception in the first place. Well, she wasn't there and I had a fine time without her. I'm ready to try new things and put myself out there."

"Good attitude, Larry. Life offers many experiences when you're ready for them. It feels good when strangers accept you and value you. You deserve it."

"I know I'm a good person," he said, "but in social situations, I'm afraid of rejection."

"Many people feel that way. It's helpful to understand why some people reject strangers. Often it has little to do with the stranger, but more to do with a person's distorted perception of the specific stranger."

"What do you mean?"

"A stranger may remind someone of another person with whom he's had a bad experience, so the stranger is automatically rejected."

Larry cupped his hand over his chin and appeared pensive. "So, what you're saying is that I shouldn't take it personally?"

"Exactly!"

"Well, what if they prefer someone younger or older, or better looking?" he asked.

"That's their problem, not yours. It's not your responsibility to please everyone. Be yourself—a kind, decent human being. This is a mantra I've expressed to you many times."

"I know, and it worked for me, Saturday. I am gaining confidence. Those Brazilians sure helped."

"The more positive experiences you have, the more secure you'll feel. You aren't the only person who has had negative experiences with others at times. It's best not to dwell on a bad experience when it occurs. Put it aside and review it at your convenience, if you want to bother with it at all. The next day, it probably won't even matter."

"You're a very wise woman. You've told me something, I've never forgotten."

"What was that, Larry?"

"Don't clutch rejection to my chest like a kid with a teddy-bear. I'm still working on it."

"Thanks, Larry." Cory considered her wisdom simple common sense.

"You're making great progress," Cory said at the end of his session.

She hadn't informed him that she had deliberately made an appointment with Ashley for ten minutes before the close of his session. She hoped to see if either of them recognized the other.

Cory watched Larry as he walked through the reception room. As he started to pass Ashley, he tripped over her large art portfolio. Well balanced, he caught himself from falling

Ashley said, "Oh, I'm so sorry."

"That's okay," he answered, walking away.

They had made eye contact. Cory was certain Larry would have had a conversation with her if she were the same Ashley he had met at the museum.

As for Ashley Hogan, she showed no recognition of Larry.

She traipsed into the consulting room, lugging the portfolio. "I have something for you. I hope you like these," she said, removing several mounted drawings. "They're yours. If you like them, I'll have them framed."

"This is a real treat. Thank you," Cory replied. She examined six of the finely executed drawings and marveled at the quality work. "These are excellent, Ashley. They must be valuable."

"I don't know about that. It's my way of saying thanks for your help," Ashley said.

"I appreciate this very much. Did you draw them from your imagination?"

"Yes, Cory, I did."

"Perfect! We'll use your work to help jog your memory. We'll go through each of these drawings to see what comes to mind."

Ashley sat at the edge of her seat. "I'm ready." She rubbed her hands together.

Cory placed the artwork on the table in front of the couch. She sat, patting the seat next to her.

Ashley followed Cory's silent command, leaned forward, and turned to the first drawing depicting a large Victorian house perched on a hill. A single giant palm tree, drawn larger than the house, suggested the house was a distance from the artist's perspective.

"Where is the house located," Cory asked.

"Since it's a Victorian, it could be anywhere in the states, but the tree suggests California."

"How did you feel when you drew the picture?"

"I'm always happy when I sketch," Ashley said.

Cory felt frustrated, but determined. "Who lives in the house?"

"I'm going to guess, two old spinsters," Ashley said. "Perhaps I remembered this from an old movie."

"Could be. Does it conjure up any feelings about it? Do you remember living in a similar house?"

Ashley closed her eyes and paused in contemplation, seemingly probing her lost memory.

"Sorry, Cory. I'm drawing a blank. It's not working."

"Okay, let's move on." She turned to a sketch of an elm tree.

"Yes. This is a rare elm. I can place it in San Francisco."

"Pretend you are there now."

Ashley closed her eyes, and took several deep breaths before speaking. "I'm strolling in Golden Gate Park. I spy a magnificent elm tree. I'm overwhelmed with joy. So many elms have died from a disease. I sit on a bench facing the wonderful tree. I open my backpack; fetch my sketchpad and charcoal pencil. I'm eager to capture the image on paper. I work steadily, enjoying every moment—it's like being in a trance.

Suddenly, I feel someone's eyes on me. I look up at a smiling man. He looks like he's enjoying watching my drawing process. When I finish, he approaches me. "Excuse me. I'm an artist, too. May I have a look at your sketch?" he asks. I show it to him. He examines it and nods. You have real talent. Where are you studying? "

Suddenly, Ashley grimaced. "Oh, I can't do this. I'm not getting where I want to be!" she moaned.

"You were doing fine. What made you stop?" Cory asked.

"I don't know," she whispered.

"Were you frightened?" Cory asked

Ashley started to cry. "No, I wasn't frightened, at least not of the nice man. He was genuine."

"When you recalled the situation, something about it may have scared you. You felt the need to stop, perhaps because it was too painful to remember the man or your art studies."

Ashley folded her arms across her chest. "It's all too frustrating."

Cory nodded. "You're experiencing a very unusual and difficult situation. It's natural to become impatient, but your bits and pieces of memory are potential clues. Right now, it's a giant jigsaw puzzle, but I assure you that cases like yours do clear up," Cory counseled.

"Are you telling me to be patient and brave?"

"Yes. When you experience an obstacle, it may be the very thing that must be removed for all of it to come together. Let's try something. Take out your sketchpad and pencil and draw the nice man in the park."

"Right now?"

"Yes, please."

Ashley did as instructed. Rapidly, she sketched an outline of the man's face and began to fill in the features. "It's all coming back. His name is Herb Wasserman. He was a fine artist, originally from New York, where he studied at the Art Students League. He also studied in Paris. He was a large man, and old enough to be my grandfather. He had a kind heart, a great sense of humor, and was very supportive of me and of my work. He introduced me to many interesting artists." She paused. "It's odd to remember so much of this slice of my life, but nothing else."

"It's one of the many pieces that will help restore your memory."

"I do believe it and I feel so much better, now that I see some progress."

"Ashley, I think your art will help fill in more pieces. It rewards you in many ways. Perhaps you should consider locating Herb Wasserman. It's possible he could help restore more of your memories."

Ashley stood. "That feels right. I'm ready. Let's go for it!"

They logged on to the Internet from Cory's computer and posted Herb's full name. In a few seconds, a news article from The San Francisco Chronicle popped up:

> WASSERMAN, Herbert – A fine San Francisco painter. A large man in every way, wonderfully witty, with keen intelligence and a well-developed sense of the ridiculous. A well-loved resident of Potrero Hill for 40 years. Died at home March 15, at age 77. Born July 7, 1925, in New York City. During Army service in World War II, he was in the pivotal Battle of the Bulge. He didn't talk about his combat experiences after the war, but was an avid collector of military and historic mementos. He attended the Art Students League of New York from 1947-1949 and studied at the *Academie de la Grande Chaumiere* in Paris from 1950 to 1952. When he came to San Francisco in 1953, he was part of the extraordinary group of gifted artists who came together around the old School of Fine Arts (now the San Francisco Art Institute) on Russian Hill and found studios and apartments with cheap rents in 1950s' North Beach. He was a founding partner of the Triangle Gallery on Columbus Avenue. Herby was a most congenial man. A wide circle of adoring friends and family will very much miss the pleasure of his company.

Ashley gasped. "Oh, how awful! He was a really good guy. How sad for his loved ones!"

"You're a compassionate person, Ashley. It's sad for those close to him, but also because we hoped he'd jog your memory. Nevertheless, your visit to San Francisco and that familiar Victorian house you sketched could be productive," Cory said.

Ashley nodded. "Yes, I do feel drawn to the area."

"It's the best reason to go there," Cory replied.

Ashley seemed to perk up. "Yes, yes. I'm sure it'd help. I feel an urgency to go there right away. I sense it's where I was happiest. I'll visit galleries, art exhibits, and cafes. I feel absolutely certain it will help me."

"It's a short flight to San Francisco and I think you'll know your way around. If not, you'll learn. Please keep in touch with me while you're there."

"I'll call every day with an update. The Inn will probably store my stuff for a fee. I'll grab some clothes and get a ticket. Oh, I'm so excited. I feel terrific." She clapped her hands. "Thanks, Cory. You're an angel."

"Can't be. I have no halo." Cory smiled.

Cory's expectations for the restoration of Ashley's memory grew. She wondered about the traumatic experience that had caused her amnesia, but she was confident whatever it was, with help, Ashley would have the strength to handle it.

⚏22⚏

Rita was missing for almost a week before her disappearance was finally mentioned in the media. Details were sparse—insufficient to grab any attention.

Cory requested Rita's office manager to create and distribute flyers throughout Del Mar, Solana Beach, Cardiff, La Jolla, and Encinitas—the local beach cafés and shop windows.

The flyer entitled "MISSING" showed an enlarged photo of "Rita Rivers, sponsor of the upcoming fun run benefit." She instructed the agreeable manager to include the phone number of the department of missing persons on the flyer.

Kitty had become a guest in Cory's house and adjusted well to the change. Both guest and host were happy with the arrangement. Kitty hid under Cory's bed whenever she heard a knock on the door, but would crawl out when called.

Cory pondered Rita's disappearance, but had no clues until she was stopped on her stroll to work by a neighbor down the street.

"I'm confused, the handsome white-haired, blue-eyed man said. I thought you were the woman who disappeared. You sure look alike."

"I suppose from a distance, there are similarities. We're both tall, slender, and have straight black hair and dark eyes. Rita is my next door neighbor."

"Then you must be Doctor Cory Cohen, our local shrink."

"Yes, I'm Cory. What's your name?"

"I'm Don Koppel. No relation to Ted. Remember him, the news guy?"

"Yes. Pleased to meet you, Don."

"That Rita sure is a swell neighbor. And charitable, too. I ran in the race she sponsored for disabled kids," Don said.

"Glad to hear it. I ran, too."

"I don't recall seeing you there. You're hard to miss. I always notice a good-looking woman."

Cory smiled. "Thanks, Don. There were hundreds of good-looking women there. It's your bonus for participating."

"Do you think it's the reason so many men run the race?" Don asked.

"It's a healthy and fun way to give to charity." Cory replied.

"So, tell me, what do you think happened to Rita? An unhappy client? A former boyfriend?"

Cory shrugged. "I wish I knew."

"Well, if there is anything I can do, please let me know," Don said.

Don's openness and warmth made a positive impression on Cory. Perhaps she could enlist his help.

"Rita's disappearance should concern our neighborhood. I believe she was taken captive from here. We must make an effort to be alert to our surroundings—to pay attention. If you see anything or anyone who looks suspicious, please call nine-one-one immediately." She paused to reflect. "As a matter of fact, would you like to help start a neighborhood watch group?"

"Oh, sure. I'd like that. I'm retired and have lots of free time to put to good use. Hey, come to think of it, I did have a suspicious caller. Someone asked me for Rita's address."

A chill rushed down Cory's spine. "Can you describe the person?"

"Gosh darn, I didn't get a good look. She was plain, middle-age."

"When did this happen?" Cory asked.

" Um. Let me see. It was when I was on my way to play chess with John around the corner. Do you know John?"

"No," Cory said.

"Well, that would make it four days ago. No, wait. John changed the date. It was two or three days ago. I'm sorry I can't remember. Since I retired, one day is much the same as the next. If it's important, I'll ask John. I do know what time it was because we always play in the early afternoon before we go out to dinner.

"It must have been her car that I saw parked a few doors down. Most visitors park in driveways, you know, unless they're strangers."

"Don, can you describe the car?"

"Why is it important?"

"It may be related to Rita's disappearance," Cory replied

"Oh-me! Oh- my!. I'll work on it."

"You'll be a hero if you remember and write down all the details before you call missing persons." She handed him a few flyers. "The number is on this flyer. Tell whoever answers whatever you remember. Please call right away, while the memory is fresh."

"Okay. My daily constitutional can wait until later. This is more important. Sometimes when I forget something, I sit down, close my eyes, and it usually comes back to me. Let's hope it does now. When I have it, I'll write it down and do just as you asked."

"Perfect." Cory smiled. "Maybe we can arrange a time to walk together."

"That'd be nice," Don said.

"Too bad it takes a grim situation to bring folks together," she replied.

Cory figured the person looking for Rita was the same woman Mimi had mentioned. With luck, Don Koppel would recall more details about the woman and her car. He'd likely have had a sharper memory of her if she were young and attractive. She cautioned herself to stop stereotyping.

* * *

Several days had passed since Ashley embarked on her mission to San Francisco.

She had called Cory shortly after her arrival to say she felt great and her geographical memories of the city had returned. All else in her memory bank remained elusive. As promised, she checked in with a daily report.

With a light office schedule, Cory was in no hurry to go home. Kitty was used to being left alone, and seemed content to play with an old tennis ball at Cory's house.

The waiting room was cluttered with old magazines and the plants needed water and food. Cory replenished the plants and stacked a few of the most recent magazines into a neat pile. She carried an armload of older magazines to her car and placed them into an empty carton in the trunk, planning to donate it to the hospital when she was in the vicinity.

She heard the ringing of her office phone and ran to answer, but by the time she'd grabbed it, Ashley had left a message:

"I'm still in San Francisco and feel very much at home. I'm staying at a small hotel near the wharf because it's easy to get to most places by foot from here—if you like to walk as I do. You were so very right. Everything is familiar to me. I know how to get around. I located the Victorian house on Telegraph Hill. When I got there, I remembered painting a picture of it that I had sold to the residents. I'm hanging around North Beach most of the time, hoping to see a familiar face or one that finds mine familiar. I've been to City Lights Bookstore every day at different times, but no luck so far. I've even tried Tai Chi in Washington Square Park. I'll check out all the Union Square galleries later. Tomorrow, it's back to Golden Gate Park. I'll call as promised." Ashley sounded very upbeat.

Cory figured that Ashley's flight from a place where she was severely traumatized to one that brought back good memories was certain to be beneficial. She felt confident that Ashley's amnesia would soon vanish and she'd work through her trauma.

Plagued by worry over Ben, Cory didn't know where to turn for information about him. The last time they had spoken together, he was in London. If anything happened to him, she had no way of learning about it, unless it was important enough to be reported in the Times.

Cory recalled her successful search on the Internet for Herb Wasserman. Perhaps she would be successful again. She logged on to the Internet and Times of London, UK news, and started to enter Ben's name, but a sudden wave of panic held her back.

Who knew what lurked in the world of cyberspace? Who knew what danger a few strokes on a keyboard might evoke?

Immediately, she knew from where her expectation of peril came. Worry over Ben had clouded her judgment. This would not do. His investigative work had become a detriment to their relationship. Together and apart, they had experienced the thrills of the chase and of the capture. Cory had enough. Flirting with danger was no longer her mode, but Ben enjoyed his career and probably wasn't ready to give it up for her. Was she ready to announce her decision?

In the past, he had contacted her at least weekly, either by phone or email. Worried, she had offered to travel to anywhere in Europe to be with him if he was ill, or had an accident, but he hadn't responded to her offer.

Why hadn't he written a few words to her to allay her anxiety? She didn't know where to turn for answers. She would just have to wait. As anxiety grew, she thought of the difficulties military families confront, but at least, as tough as it was, they had the support and comfort of a community and could rely on news. Cory wouldn't burden her friends and she had nowhere to turn for news of Ben.

Although she valued her relationship with Ben, her apprehension over his welfare had robbed her of sleep for the past few nights. During the days she was distracted by concentration on her few patients; but toward evening, although tired, sleep eluded her. A bit of comfort came from Kitty who had claimed a place on Cory's bed.

The joy she had experienced with Ben wasn't worth the anxiety and sleepless nights.

She decided to tell him that their relationship was in crisis, and she would commit to it on the condition that he would not accept any dangerous assignments.

Her life before she met him was fulfilling. She enjoyed the companionship of a few friends, and was content on her own, welcoming solitude as one of her three "R's"—relax, read, and reflect. She was never bored. She enjoyed her collection of recorded jazz and classical music, a good book, a film, and surfing the Internet in that order.

Since Ben was in the U.K., she frequently watched BBC News online before checking her email. There wasn't any news in the UK that she could reasonably link to Ben. She figured it unlikely that the matter he was investigating was newsworthy.

She clicked on her email that was replete with postings from colleagues, political activist groups, and jokes from distant friends. It kept her in the loop, but it would take up too much time and she was impatient. Her mission was to check for any emails from Ben, but there wasn't any.

Cory posted a single message:

Ben,
Since you haven't responded to my last message, my apprehension over your welfare has become unbearable. I can't tolerate worry as a bed companion, robbing me of sleep.

Please reply ASAP.
Cory

She filed away her daily notes and locked the cabinet.

As she stepped out the front door of her office, she tripped and almost fell over a neatly wrapped square package with a bow on it. A card with her name boldly printed was clipped to the red satin bow. At first she smiled with pleasure, but a brief examination gave her no information about the sender. Very odd, she thought. It must have been placed there soon after she returned from the magazine chore. Why didn't the delivery person ring the bell and attempt to hand the package to her personally?

Suddenly, she froze in fear. The package could contain something dangerous—maybe an explosive! Better to be safe than sorry. She punched in 911, provided her name and address, and described the suspicious package outside her door. "It may be a bomb," she said with a tremor in her voice.

"Don't touch it. Hurry. Leave the area now," the officer commanded.

Her heart raced as she ran to her car, jumped in and drove towards home. Within a few minutes, she heard a siren.

Why would someone do this to her? Had she unintentionally angered someone—someone so disturbed as to go to such lengths for retribution?

No one in her current caseload came to mind. Paranoid and delusional patients, those with thought disorders are most apt to misinterpret the words or mannerisms of others. Many tend to keep grudges for many years.

About twenty years ago, she had treated a depressed, angry woman who initially presented in a polite, pleasant fashion, but gradually anger and paranoia emerged. Concerned by the woman's erratic mood swings, Cory referred her to a psychiatrist for medication.

Several years later, the same patient reported that psychiatrist to the police and the Medical Board, claiming he was in love with her and had broken into her home and stolen a valuable portrait of her. It wasn't unusual for paranoid patients to have delusions of grandeur. There was no evidence to support her complaint. The story made headlines and alarmed the mental health community.

There was a possibility that the person who had left the suspicious package was someone involved in Ashley's trauma. Perhaps that person had followed Ashley to Cory's office and was determined to prevent her from helping Ashley. Maybe it was the same person who had shot at her outside the Healthy Touch Massage Salon and had mistakenly snatched Rita, thinking she was Cory.

And then there was "Carole Roy", the attempted blackmailer, whose outrageous legal claim seemed to evaporate after it was ignored. Had she or he found another way to frighten her, to get even for having failed in the blackmail threat?

For a few moments, Cory toyed with the notion, but abandoned it. Most likely Roy's motive was financial gain, not revenge.

It was the sheriff's job to uncover a suspect. Cory could only hypothesize.

About an hour later, Cory's doorbell rang. She peered out the peephole and saw the sheriff's car parked in her driveway. A uniformed officer stood outside her door. Evidently, he had tracked Cory to her home.

She opened the door and invited the deputy sheriff inside. He was a tall, muscular young man with short reddish blonde color and freckles.

"I'm Deputy Jim McDonald," he said. "Did you call about a suspicious package today?"

"Yes," Cory replied. "I appreciate your quick response. What did you find?

"Let me reassure you. It wasn't an explosive."

"Phew! I'm sorry I had to bother you."

"We're trained for this. It's good practice. Would you like to know the contents of the package?"

"Of course," Cory said.

"Your suspicious package contained a box of thawed Healthy Choice cake."

Cory burst out laughing. "Oh! What a hoot! I'm pretty sure I know who left it. Very recently I advised a patient to make healthy choices. I should have said, "healthy decisions." She misunderstood and thought I meant the food. Obviously, she was angrier at me than I realized."

The officer chuckled. "We get plenty of unusual cases, but this one sure takes the cake—no pun intended! Do you want to file charges?"

"What would that entail?"

"Evidence. Your statement. Her fingerprints."

"She said she spent time in jail, so her prints are on file. I'd rather not add fuel to her anger."

"It may teach her a lesson and prevent her from bothering you again."

"I think it may cause more harm than good," Cory said.

"A suspicious package may be the start of a vindictive rampage. Who knows what she'll do next? Next time may not be so innocent."

Cory nodded. "Makes sense. I'll follow your suggestion."

He handed her a form. After scanning and signing the form, she returned it to him.

=23=

Early the next afternoon, Cory heard a knock on the door. Still unnerved from the suspicious package incident, she froze. Kitty dashed into the bedroom and slid under the bed.

Cory looked out the peephole and saw Don Koppel holding a chessboard and wooden box.

She sighed in relief and opened the door.

"Sorry to bother you, but I haven't seen you around and figured I ought to check on you," said Don.

"Thank you, Don. That is very thoughtful. Please come in and I'll brew some tea, and you can tell me about any progress with the neighborhood watch group."

She ushered Mr. Koppel into the living room, and motioned him toward Ben's favorite chair. She pointed to the chessboard and box. "If this is an invitation to play chess, I'm afraid I'm a poor match for you."

"Oh, no. I'm on way to Hank's. I promised to teach him how to play. I just stopped over to check on you and maybe have a brief chat."

"That's fine. I'm glad to see you."

Cory prepared a tea tray and a platter of assorted cookies. She placed the refreshments on the table facing Don and seated herself across from him.

"This is an unexpected treat," Don said. Thanks for your hospitality. Pleased to report that already, a few people signed up. Two—John and I—are retired and have time and energy to do something for our neighborhood. Two others are parents of kids away at school.

"And then there is Gladys Goldberg; she's two streets down— loves gardening. But don't you dare call her Gladys. She says it sounds like Glad-Ass and prefers Goldie, for Goldberg."

Cory chuckled.

"Let me tell you about Goldie. She's something else. When she noticed Hank's front yard needed work, she asked if she could help. Poor guy had a rash of bad luck, widowed last year, and then this year, he had hip replacement. His family lives far away, so he had an aide coming in for some time, but she ripped him off."

"Oh, my! That is shameful! Is he sure the aide ripped him off?" Cory asked.

"He's positive. The only other unfamiliar person that visited him was the rehab person and she never had entered the room where his precious heirlooms were stored.

"His weekly cleaning woman has worked for him for fifteen years and is honest as the day is long. The aide lived in for about two months and quit without notice. Probably she had discovered his treasure while he was asleep. He was afraid to report it until now."

"From what you've said, it does seem likely the aide is the thief." Cory poured their tea. "To work as an aide to a vulnerable person and steal from him is the ultimate *chutzpah*."

"You mean '*shanda!*'"

"Yes, Don. Shanda is a more appropriate word. I remember it means 'shame,'" Cory said. "I hope Hank reported the theft to the referral agency, and to the police."

"I advised him to report it when he told me, but he couldn't deal with it. He refused my offer to do it for him. But, Goldie—what a woman! She has a special way of reaching him. She even notified his insurance agent. It's good that he welcomed Goldie like a breath of fresh air. His garden looks great and they are bosom buddies. She fusses over him and he loves it."

"Instant companions. Easy, much like when we were kids," Cory reflected.

"Only instead of playing stick ball, they watch old movies and discuss books. A simple life spent together makes them happy. She feels important and he feels reborn.

The theft happened over a month ago, but Goldie felt so strongly over the matter, she wouldn't let go of it until she convinced Hank to report it. She said he had to prevent that *momzer* from hurting others. Goldie is a retired lawyer and practiced for many years. Hank respects her intelligence."

"Sounds like Goldie's a fine woman. She gives him what he needs—companionship and security," Cory said.

"And good sense. Oh, don't forget, she enjoys the relationship too. It makes her feel needed and important," Don remarked.

"You're very astute, Don."

Although no one was eavesdropping, Koppel leaned forward and whispered, "He told me he's sorry he didn't marry a Jewish woman."

"Come on, Don, you know not all Jewish women are alike."

"You're telling me? I should know! I divorced one. She was demanding, just like my *yiddisher* mama, but that's a story properly told on your therapy couch. Your name is Cohen. You must have married a Jewish man."

"Cohen is my father's name."

"A beauty like you is single?"

Cory grinned. "Thanks for the compliment." She didn't want to share her history with Don. He seemed to enjoy the role of neighborhood *yenta* a bit too much.

"So how many are on the committee?" she asked.

"We need seven more to make a *minyon*."

Cory frowned. "You mean we only have three people on the committee?"

"No. I was joking. We already have six people. Three include three Jews: you, me, and Goldie."

Cory shook her head. "Whenever we think we're in a minority, we start counting the Jews. Ghetto history must be in our genes."

"It gives us connection. I want you should know that I called missing persons," Don said in a Yiddish accent. "I tried giving them a description of the woman I'd seen near Rita's house before Rita went missing. They sent someone to interview me right away. Such efficiency, I've never seen from a government agency."

"Maybe it was considered a priority, or they weren't busy."

Don Koppel shrugged. "You think we have a VIP in our midst?"

"Realtor to the rich? Don't think that qualifies. Maybe the mysterious woman asking you questions went to the wrong house?"

"Or, Rita's real estate is a cover for her work as a CIA operative," Don suggested.

"You have a good imagination, Don. Were you able to provide a description of the car?"

"I got the model, vintage, and color easily. I remembered glancing at the license plate. I'm certain it wasn't a California plate."

"Maybe I can help you remember. Are you willing to try hypnosis?

"Hypnosis? Where would I have to go?"

"Right here. I'm trained in hypnosis. Sometimes I help witnesses of accidents or crimes recall details of the event. I've also had good results with pain management patients. It doesn't always work, but it's worth a try."

"Oh, my! I don't want to rush into this." He paused. "First, I should ask if there could be any lasting after effects—you know, reasons why it may not be a good thing."

"When used by a professional for a legitimate purpose, there should be no ill effects."

"I remember watching a hypnotist at a show using it with volunteers who began to cluck like chickens. After they learned what happened, some were embarrassed, frightened, and some were very angry," Don said.

"I understand. They felt exploited—used for an entertainment shtick. I'm not an entertainer. I promise our short session will be for only one purpose—to help jog your memory of the car license plate and the driver in order to help find Rita."

"I'm okay with that," Don clapped his hands. Go for it."

Don Koppel turned out to be a cooperative and excellent hypnosis subject. Within a short time, he was able to describe the woman in detail just as he had seen her when she walked over to him.

"She's wearing faded blue jeans, a white tee shirt, and brown leather boots. The toes are pointed." He wasn't sure if they were cowboy boots, but his description fit the criteria.

"Her hair is messy, a mousy color with a few strands of gray. She's wearing wrap-around yellow sunglasses—the kind that diminishes glare, like John used to wear before he had cataract surgery.

"She's medium height and weight. A light tan or gray-colored baseball cap with a wide brim is perched on her head."

Don couldn't recall any logo on the cap or tee shirt.

"I figure her age between fifty and sixty, judging from her wrinkled brow and hair. Her unkempt appearance suggests she'd been driving around for a long time."

The only distinctive feature Don noted was a deep Kirk Douglas-type cleft in her chin.

He recalled the car easily as it was a sunny afternoon and his friend owned one of the same vintage, brand, and color—a silver grey 2002 four-door Honda Civic. He struggled to resurrect the license plate. "Sheesh, the car is parked close enough for me to read the license plate, especially because the day is bright. "Ah, yes. The top portion of the plate is sunny yellow and the rest of the plate is a nice sky blue. The letter S and the numerals are dark blue."

Don squinted. "*Oy vey,* this feels like I'm at the optometrist, getting my vision checked by reading the eye chart. Let me see. Ah-hah. There are three letters and three digits, but I'm confused with the order of the letters and numbers. I think two zeros or two O's, a nine, six, and B. "

While Don described the license plate, Cory Googled her laptop for pictures of state license plates.

Bingo! Of the fifty states, Nevada's license plate matched Don's description.

The woman he pictured had to be the same person Mimi had mentioned—the one who rang her doorbell and identified herself as Lydia Brooks, a private investigator from Phoenix. It wasn't unusual for people to register a car in one state and work in an adjoining state.

"Did she give you her name?"

"Um, let me see. Yes. Linda, or Lydia Brooks. I'm not sure."

Bingo!

Cory tried to find information online about Lydia Brooks. The popular name made the task daunting. Cory suspected Lydia Brooks was an assumed name anyway. No legitimate investigator would do business in such a non-professional manner. The puzzle was too much to tackle while Don Koppel reclined on her couch with a contented smile on his face.

She allowed him a few minutes to rest before she brought him out of hypnosis.

Don yawned. "Wow, I feel like I had a good nap. He stood and stretched. That was terrific, Cory. I feel so relaxed. Maybe I should come here when I have a bout of insomnia. Don't worry, I'm only joking. I usually sleep like a baby."

Cory smiled. "You're a fine subject with an excellent visual memory. She told him what she had learned from the session.

"I sure hope it helps find Rita. With *mazel*, she'll be safe."

"Yes. Mazel—good luck. Hurry and call missing persons right away."

"I'm on my way. Thanks for the tea and the relaxation session." Don trotted out.

=24=

The next day, eager to share the suspicious package incident with a close friend, Cory called Betty, but she wasn't available. She was about to ring Joe and Roberta, when her own phone rang. It was Joe.

"You must have read my mind, Joe. I was about to phone you."

"Remember how often that happened in grad school, Cory?"

"Yes. You called it 'serendipity', and I called it 'psychic'."

Joe sighed. "Those were the days."

"I remember them well, but without the stress of school, our best days are now," Cory reflected.

"You're right, Cory. Say, I'd like to drive over and see you as soon as possible."

She was startled. Joe had never asked to visit her. Their get-togethers were usually on his turf—the beautiful, comfortable estate he and Roberta had designed together that had been her sanctuary several years ago.

"What's wrong? Is Roberta okay? Are you okay?"

"Absolutely, nothing is wrong. Don't upset yourself. It's something I have for you."

"Phew! I'm relieved. It must be a Roberta creation."

"It's a surprise. May I come over now?"

"Of course."

Cory wasn't reassured. She had detected a sense of urgency—a somber tone in Joe's voice. Perhaps she misunderstood. Maybe he wanted to plan a surprise party for Roberta and needed help. What fun that would be!

She quickly tidied the living room and swept the path outside her front door, all the while wondering what Joe could possibly have for her—if not Roberta's newest culinary treat.

She brushed her teeth, washed her face, combed her hair, and checked her image in the mirror. Good enough for an old friend, she thought.

About fifteen minutes later, Joe arrived with a large envelope in his hand. She greeted him with a hug, and led him into the living room.

Joe plopped on the couch and Cory sat on the chair facing him. "Would you like wine, tea, coffee, juice?"

"Not now, thanks, Cory. This envelope arrived today. It's addressed to me, but it contains a letter for you and one to me. It's from Ben."

Cory had a sinking sensation in the pit of her stomach.

"In his letter to me, he's asked me to personally deliver his letter to you. He explained that all his movements and communications are scrutinized. He doesn't want you to worry and needed to explain this to you. He took precaution and gave this packet to a visiting Greek friend who mailed it from Greece."

Cory's hands shook as she opened her letter and read:

> My dearest Cory,
>
> You are probably worried, concerned and angry at me for not communicating with you. Please try to understand. When I took the assignment, I expected it would be short and I'd be home soon.
>
> And it actually turned out to be brief and successful, but just as I was ready to make travel plans to return to the states from London, I came across valuable information confirming my long suspicion that my former boss is in league with an enemy agent. Obviously, I can't let this information evaporate. I'm in the process of gathering additional material to build a case.
>
> Unfortunately, it appears he suspects that I know about his involvement with the agent. He's a powerful man and thwarts me by his overwhelming surveillance on all my activities. Everywhere I go and everything I do is being scrutinized. Virtually, I'm a prisoner. He managed to put a hold on my passport using some cockamamie reason.
>
> Through my contacts, important people in our government have been informed of my predicament. Hopefully, this situation will be resolved soon. I long for a normal life with you.

Please take care of yourself and I promise the same here. I'm sorry for worrying you, but I must level with you—my dearest.

Love,

Ben

P.S. Either destroy this letter or keep it safe.

Tears rolled down her cheeks. She grabbed a tissue from a box nearby and blotted her face.

Joe leaned forward and took her hand. "In his letter to me, Ben apologized for using me as a conduit. He reasoned that I'd be here to comfort you."

She gave Joe a weak smile. "I'm afraid for him. He's a fine man. I don't want to lose him," she said.

"Life isn't fair for many people. It is rarely perfect for long. We must enjoy every precious moment," Joe said.

"I know. Damn it, Joe! I love Ben, but it is very hard to overcome the anxiety over his safety—especially after waiting so long for him to return."

Joe leaned over and took her hands in his big paws. "You're a strong person," he said. "You've suffered much worse than this temporary glitch. I remember."

"Yes. I know I've coped with many difficulties in my life, but each time a crisis erupts, I think of the best way to address it, and hope it will soon end. With Ben, there is nothing I can do to help him. I feel vulnerable—like a bird without wings."

"Ben doesn't need your help. Trust his strengths, and your own, and you'll both prevail," Joe said.

She paused in thought, unwilling to consider another option—to end the relationship. "If Ben's former boss has any information about me, maybe I should be afraid of what he might do to me."

"What do you think he'd do?"

"I don't know. I suppose he could have me killed, or tortured."

"Ben's letter frightened you, but let's be rational, Cory. First, it is doubtful Ben's former boss knows anything about you. Most likely, Ben has taken good measures to protect you—that is the reason, he didn't contact you directly for a long time. Second, what good would it do for his boss to hurt you, assuming he did know of you?"

"Revenge," Cory said. She crossed her arms across her chest, and shivered.

"He's too smart and too busy for that. He just wants to thwart Ben and to save his own sorry ass," Joe said.

"I sure hope you're right."

She considered telling Joe about the shooting and her missing neighbor, but he would insist she move in with him and Roberta. Maybe it would be the safest thing to do, but she felt more comfortable on her own turf, and closer to her office.

Joe glanced at his wristwatch.

"Roberta left the house some time ago. She's probably finished checking the so-called antiques at that inn in Cardiff and on her way to peek into a few galleries on US-101 in Encinitas, by now. She promised to call to see if you'll join us when she's finished."

"I'd like that, Joe. I always enjoy being with both of you, but especially now. Solitude doesn't feel right today."

Joe leaned forward and hugged her. "I know you do very well alone, but in a crisis, friends are the best buffer. And besides, we enjoy being with you. We're like a family we handpicked—and our long history we share."

"You know I'm ever so grateful for it," Cory said, hugging Joe harder.

He released her. "When I called today, you mentioned you were about to call me. Did you have something special to talk about?"

Cory smiled. "I'm glad to change the subject. Yes. I had something funny to tell you." She recounted the Healthy Choice session with Elena and the subsequent suspicious package incident.

Joe laughed and was still laughing when his mobile phone jingled.

"Hi, Hon. Yes, I am laughing. Oh, well, Cory just told me something funny that happened to her. She'll tell you later. Where should we meet you? O.K. Ten minutes or so."

"Let's take my car," Joe said. "If you want company, we'll stay here with you tonight or at our place. Right now, we're off to the Pannikin in Encinitas."

"We'll see how it goes," Cory said, grabbing her purse and jacket. She set the security alarm and locked the door.

The short drive along the coast relaxed her. She considered herself a lucky woman to have good, caring friends, always available when she needed them.

Joe slid the car into a parking space at the Pannikin, a popular café converted from a vintage house where bikers, beach-goers and locals enjoyed a repast of coffee and delectable, wholesome food in a relaxing atmosphere.

Seated on the porch dining area, Roberta had spread the local newspaper on the table. The two vacant seats on either side of her clearly signaled she was either expecting friends or in no mood to share her space with strangers.

The two women kissed each other on their cheeks, and gabbed about current events. They agreed that politics and the media were hot button topics best shared with likeminded friends.

"Sometimes patients open a session with a remark about politics, and I force myself to resist agreeing," Cory said. "And if they support measures that I find offensive, I remind myself they're my patients, not members of the wrong-headed party."

Joe chimed in. "It's inappropriate to discuss politics with patients—even those with whom we agree. Consider it a patient's resistance to therapy, Cory, and change the subject, quickly."

"I try, but sometimes they're so passionate about a political situation and seem desperate to vent. Their concerns are present and real—not an overreaction—not misplaced anger—not always resistance. I often feel as they do and want to commiserate and talk about how they could serve their cause; but is psychotherapy the proper venue? Patients want to be understood. If I ignore their discontent, I'm not helping them," Cory said. "It's a dilemma."

"Find a way that doesn't involve politics. Maybe we should plan a program for therapists during election years to discuss this situation," Joe suggested.

Cory nodded. "I think we'd have a full house of like-minded folks."

"If you're finished with your professional dialogue, I have some professional stuff of my own to share," Roberta said.

"We're listening," said Joe and Cory in unison.

"You remember telling me about the hotel in Cardiff that featured antique reproductions in the lobby? You had asked me how to detect a genuine antique from a copy."

Cory nodded.

"Well, I was curious so I went there to see the collection."

"And?" Cory asked

"I'm glad you mentioned it, Cory. The stuff struck me as superb reproductions with a single exception—a wall tapestry. It's quite amazing. I remember bidding on an identical piece at Christie's in New York—at least it was very much like it. It was an English Pastoral tapestry, probably late 17th century, in the manner of Francis Cleyn. Probably worth in the neighborhood of thirty grand."

"Wow! Your knowledge astounds me, Ro."

Roberta smiled. "Madeline Michel, a well-known sculptor and antique collector, outbid me. She told me she was happy to meet someone who appreciated the piece as much as she did. That gracious, lovely lady invited me to tea."

"Did you go?"

"Naturally. We had a delightful time together. She was leaving for Paris the next day. We exchanged phone numbers and she promised to call me when she returned, but I've never heard from her. *C'est la vie!*"

"Maybe she lost your number. Have you tried to call her?" Joe asked.

"It's been quite a while since we met, and I'm not sure that I still have her card," Roberta said.

"It may be uncomfortable to call someone who promised to call you, but didn't," Cory offered.

"Actually, I had almost forgotten about her until I saw that tapestry."

"How in the world would a precious art object land on the wall at an inn here?" asked Cory.

Roberta shrugged. "I asked myself the same question."

Joe looked at Cory. "How would you solve this puzzle?"

"If I were Roberta and could reach Madeline Michel, I'd tell her about my shocking discovery of the tapestry hanging on a wall of an otherwise mundane beach hotel. I'd say I identified it as either an original or a splendid reproduction of a 17th century whatcha-ma-callit tapestry—a piece for which we both had bid at a Christie's auction in New York. When I saw it, I immediately thought of her and thought she should know about it in case it had been stolen, lost, sold, or reproduced. I'd say I called to reconnect with her and to clear up a mystery."

"She'd probably consider me a con-artist," Ro mumbled.

"Why?" Cory asked.

"Savvy collectors are suspicious."

"Well, then I'd get in touch with the company that furnishes the hotel and ask them if the tapestry is a reproduction. Is that a better idea?"

"Curiosity killed the cat," Joe said.

"If people weren't curious, we wouldn't have all the good stuff that comes from science. We live better because of curiosity," Cory replied like a defensive sophomore.

"True. Apart from psychology, your curiosity often puts you in danger," Joe said.

"Duly noted, Joe."

He rose from his chair. "The aroma from the kitchen beckons. Do you want menus, or shall I go to the counter and order for us?"

Awaiting Roberta's response, Cory turned her head to Roberta.

"Surprise us, hon," Roberta said as Joe went off to order. She leaned closer to Cory and said softly, "That tapestry really bugs me."

"A call to that collector really is appropriate," Cory whispered.

"You're right, Cory. Madeline Michel is a fascinating person and I'd like to keep in touch with her, anyway." She paused, cupped her chin in her hand and appeared deep in thought.

"It just dawned on me where I stashed her card," Roberta said, rubbing her hands together as though preparing a culinary treat.

After lunch, they lounged around making small talk. Joe asked Cory three times, and Roberta asked four times, if she wanted to spend the night at their house.

"We could stay up all night and have a pajama party and play games, like old times," Roberta said.

"I've got too much on my mind now, but I'll take a rain check."

"*Mi casa es su casa*," Roberta sang.

"For that, I'm blessed."

As Cory and Roberta walked arm in arm toward the car, Cory said, "Let me know the outcome of your call to MM."

⋰25⋱

When Cory opened her front door, she spied her cell phone on the table. In her haste to leave with Joe, she had forgotten to disconnect it from the charger. Ben's upsetting letter had distracted her. She vowed to be more alert. A glance at the phone showed no messages.

Kitty, craving attention, ran to her current keeper. Cory cuddled her, stroked her soft white fur while Kitty purred her response.

Rita had adopted Kitty as a kitten from an animal rescue center and provided her with fresh fish in season and the finest cat food and toys, and an abundance of affection.

Cory hoped Rita was safe and unhurt and would realize that Kitty had good care, despite the absence of fresh fish. Kitty sniffed at and promptly rejected canned tuna. She would rather walk away hungry than compromise her values. Cory couldn't watch Kitty starve, so she purchased enriched dry food made especially for indulgent cat-lovers, which the fussy feline accepted after some reluctance.

Apart from Kitty's expensive food preferences, she and Cory enjoyed their new comforting, symbiotic relationship.

With Kitty purring on her lap, Cory sat on the couch, brooding over Ben's precarious situation. She wondered about a possible connection to Rita's disappearance. Would an inept investigator have mistaken Rita for Cory and snatched her to parts unknown as a threat or for some type of ransom?

If Rita's disappearance was a case of mistaken identity, Ben should have received a threat informing him that if he tries to harm his superior, Cory will be a victim. Maybe Ben received such a threat, but didn't want to frighten her and kept it to himself.

If Rita was snatched by mistake and could prove her identity, would the culprit release her? Not if her captive feared a dangerous response. Cory shuddered at the thought of innocent Rita in such a perilous position.

It was time to water Rita's indoor plants—and an opportunity to investigate. Cory fetched Rita's keys and entered her house.

The prospect of snooping in Rita's private domain made Cory uncomfortable, but waiting an indeterminate time for a Missing Persons investigator to show up was a worse option.

Cory wondered if she was rationalizing to herself, claiming impatience, or succumbing to garden-variety curiosity? *Stop this incessant self-analysis. Investigation is necessary. Go for it!* she told herself.

She filled the watering pitcher with plant food and water, and set it on the kitchen counter, while she poked around in Rita's bedroom.

Upon stepping into the walk-in closet, she tripped and fell over Rita's large handbag, landing on her backside. Resting on the floor, she rubbed her behind and examined her bruised arms and legs, muttering to herself, "Curiosity killed the cat." Ignoring the pain and warning, she seized the chance to rummage through the purse.

She pulled out an alligator leather wallet. It contained a California driver license, several credit cards, and six twenty-dollar bills. She returned the items to their respective places.

Cory recalled that before Rita's disappearance, she was seen jogging in the neighborhood.

Few women carry wallets while jogging close to home. If they plan to make a local purchase, they would pocket a credit card or a few bills.

If Rita had been snatched by mistake, she would probably have nothing on her to prove her identity.

With some discomfort, she hobbled over to Rita's desk and opened the top drawer. She pulled out a large manila envelope. Inside were ten photos of a little boy at various stages of his development—from birth up until age ten, according to the notations on the back of each photo.

His name was Mark. He had thick black hair, sad brown eyes with long eyelashes, a dark complexion, and a sweet smile.

In the most recent dated photo, Mark stood outside the Nevada School for Mentally Challenged Children. As Cory examined the photo, a lump of sadness formed in her throat.

She figured the school must be one of Rita's charities, and the boy, someone special to her.

Upon further inspection, Cory found a Nevada driver's license issued to Maria Rivera. The photo bore a close resemblance to Rita. Cory compared the Nevada and California licenses and noticed the month and day were identical on both, but the year was ten years earlier on Maria's than Rita's.

A birth certificate for Mark Marcos Rivera listed his parents as Maria and Marcos Rivera.

The names were familiar, rather common in the nearby Mexican community.

Cory conjured up a possible scenario—one she had heard many times in her career:

Rita, alias Maria, escaped from her abusive husband Marcos, probably after their mentally challenged son was placed into an institution.

She relocated to California, had cosmetic surgery, and assumed a new identity.

Marcos located her through the investigator, probably the woman Don had encountered. Marcos used the information to capture his son's mother.

Rita's disappearance probably had nothing to do with Ben's enemy. The shooter probably had mistaken Cory for Rita, not the other way around.

Cory dashed home to call Missing Persons.

Before she picked up the phone, she noticed two messages had arrived while she was out snooping.

Betty sounded cheerful. Ashley sounded distressed.

Cory called Missing Persons, left a detailed message expressing urgency, and asked for a call back. She provided her cell and home phone numbers.

Next, she returned Ashley's call.

"My visit to San Francisco has proven productive. I've remembered my life here, but there is still a huge cloud hiding my life before that time. Most disturbing to me is that chunk of time missing between San Francisco and the first time we met. Isn't that strange?" Ashley asked.

"Your memory is like a jig saw puzzle that fell out of the box, the pieces scattered all around. We found some pieces that fit together, but we need to find the rest.

"I get it. I'm returning to San Diego tomorrow. The Inn has my old room ready for me. I'd like to see you as soon as possible. This time I'm determined to try hypnosis again."

"Fine. Call me when you've settled in, and we'll make an appointment."

"Thanks, Cory."

Cory wanted to share the news of Ben with Betty, but she wouldn't do it on the phone. She preferred to talk about other happenings.

When Betty picked up, Cory related the suspicious package incident, expecting her to laugh, but instead Betty's voice sounded alarmed.

"You were in danger. That's very frightening."

"I assure you, Betty, no harm was done."

"Yes, but it scared you, didn't it?"

"It's over now. I don't think that woman will bother me again—not after the sheriff has warned her."

"You can't be sure. That could make her angrier and she may try to pull something worse on you. You know paranoids can be dangerous. I wonder why you're a magnet for troublesome patients."

"We're psychologists. I feel privileged to work with most of my patients. I don't deliberately select troublesome ones." There was hurt in Cory's voice.

"I'm sorry, Cory. I just get worried about you sometimes. Please don't fault me for being overprotective, given your history."

"Please give me credit for my ability to take care of myself, Betty."

"I do. I'm sorry if I hurt you, Cory."

"Don't worry about it."

"Look, I was on my way out to do a few errands up your way. Can I come over in an hour?"

"Sure, Bet."

* * *

Forty-five minutes later, Betty was at the door, bearing a quart of Cory's favorite lactose-free vanilla ice cream.

Cory scooped the dessert into two bowls and tossed in some fresh strawberries. They sat in the cozy kitchen booth.

"Listen, my dear friend," Cory announced. I have a very special treat for us. A colleague rewarded me with two gift certificates to Palliative, a world famous spa. It includes all the services plus lunch."

"Wow, that's quite a treat. That spa is very expensive."

"He can afford it. He doesn't take insurance and has wealthy clients."

"But why did he give you a gift? It's not your birthday."

"I may have saved his career. He's very well-trained, and a popular psychotherapy supervisor, but his sloppy business practices could jeopardize his practice."

"Who is he and how did you get involved with him?" Betty asked, her face registering maternal concern.

Cory related the blackmail threats while Betty sat transfixed.

"I know it's not your fault, Cory, but you seem to be a magnet for danger. And your new attractive, generous, wealthy colleague may be in the same camp. By the way, is he single?"

"I'm not sure. He mentioned that he offers continuing education courses with his partner, Kurt. I suspect they are a couple since his note that came with the gift said he and Kurt are regulars at the spa."

"Ah, hah. The guys that interest me are always attached."

"You know that isn't accidental, Betty."

"Yes, Doctor. Of that I am aware. With all the therapy I've had, that part of my psyche appears to be etched in concrete."

The conversation was all too familiar and never fruitful. Cory chose to change the subject.

"Listen to this. It's a real puzzle: Three successful colleagues, each with a masculine first name, are targeted by a blackmailer claiming to be their former patient. But none of the psychologists ever treated anyone by that name. Is the miscreant a paranoid person who imagines rejection from male psychologists?"

"Could be," Betty said. "Or she figures male professionals are ripe for and may fear accusations of sexual misconduct."

"Assuming the blackmailer is a woman. Can't tell by the name. The blackmailer's name may be deliberately ambiguous. The two guys hit by this scheme got the threat from someone whose first and last names could be interchanged."

"This may be a coincidence, but you, dear Cory, are always looking to solve a mystery."

"I accept the criticism."

"A statement, Cory. Not a criticism."

"Accepted as such. Let's use this gift. We'll take a leisurely drive, and enjoy a full day of pampering, including lunch. When would you like to go?"

"As soon as possible," Betty said. "Let's check our calendars and discuss it after I get home." She rinsed the dessert bowls and stored them in the empty dishwasher.

Fifteen minutes after Betty left, Cory's doorbell rang. She looked through the peephole and saw the face of a uniformed woman.

"I'm from Missing Persons," the investigator announced as she slid a card under the door.

Cory grabbed Rita's keys, opened the door, and stepped out.

"The missing woman is my next-door neighbor." She beckoned the investigator to follow her to Rita's house.

Cory spied the watering can on Rita's kitchen counter.

"When I came here to tend to the plants, I took the opportunity to investigate, hoping to find a lead to my neighbor's disappearance."

As Cory handed the large manila envelope to the investigator, she said, "In my work as a psychologist, I've treated many abused women who had escaped and were forced to start life anew. Given the documents in this envelope, I think it's possible that Rita may have been such a victim. It is possible that she may be the mother of the boy in the photo.

"Rita sponsored a charity for mentally challenged children, and organized a popular annual run. I may be wrong, but the evidence in this envelope fits my hypothesis." She handed the investigator Rita's wallet containing her California driver's license.

The investigator took all the materials that supported Cory's hypothesis. She thanked Cory and departed without an accusatory word.

≈26≈

Cory awoke suddenly and glanced at the illuminated clock on her bedside table. It read 3:00AM. She wasn't sure what had awakened her. Rita was on her mind before she had fallen asleep. Perhaps she had a bad dream about her, but she couldn't recall it.

She jotted a note to herself to follow up on the investigation of Rita's disappearance.

Later that morning, Don Koppel rang her doorbell. She promptly opened the door.

"I was out taking my morning walk and decided to drop in on you to keep you up to speed on our neighborhood watch team."

She ushered him into the kitchen. "I was just having breakfast. Please join me."

"Just coffee, please. I'm here with some disturbing neighborhood news."

Cory shuddered. "Oh, my. What is it, Don?"

"We have a strange, reclusive neighbor just a few doors down from Hank's house. Bill is the backyard neighbor of the recluse. He related an odd incident. Once Bill happened to be outside, weeding his garden at the same time as that neighbor.

Evidentially, the recluse hadn't noticed him until Bill called out and waved to him. Instead of acknowledging him, as most normal folks would do, his eccentric neighbor dashed inside."

"Maybe, he's deaf, or he had a nature call," Cory conjectured.

"He's not deaf. There is more. Just the other day, a Girl Scout and her mom were out selling cookies. When the kid rang his doorbell, he wouldn't open the door, but yelled, "Get the hell out of here. I don't want any snoops bothering me.""

"A distressing experience for a little kid," Cory said, handing Don a cup of freshly brewed coffee. "The guy sounds a bit paranoid."

"*Mishuga*," if you ask me, Don said

Cory nodded. She carried a plate of wheat toast and blackberry jam into the kitchen booth and beckoned him to follow.

"Why, thank you dear neighbor," he said. "This sure is cozy. Seems like you're always feeding me. I'd like to reciprocate. How about I take you to lunch one day this week?"

"Thank you. That'd be fun," Cory said. "I'm free at lunchtime tomorrow."

"Okay. We'll meet at the neighborhood café at noon. Now, let me tell you about Goldie. One night when she had insomnia, she marched around the neighborhood, hoping it would tire her enough to sleep."

"Brave woman," Cory said.

"She's very smart and very cautious. When she walks in the wee hours, she wears a whistle attached to a cord around her neck. She carries her cell phone in her pocket, and if needed, the heavy flashlight in her hand could serve as a serious weapon. Goldie's prepared. Anyway, she was pretty sure that she heard a woman crying and moaning from inside a house."

"Believe me, Goldie has chutzpah. With her ear pressed on the front door, she clearly defined the sounds as painful moans. Don't you think we should notify the sheriff?" Don asked.

"I doubt what she heard constitutes evidence of foul play. Maybe the man is taking care of an ailing spouse, or a housemate. I think it'd be a good idea for us to take turns patrolling the neighborhood twenty-four seven, if possible. If anyone sees or hears anything suspicious, then we should call nine-one-one," Cory said.

"So, you think we need more to suggest something unsavory is occurring inside his house?"

Cory nodded.

"O.K. We now have sufficient volunteers. I'll call an emergency meeting for eight o'clock tonight at Hank's house. His is the most accommodating place for a large meeting. First, I'll run it by Goldie and Hank—and I'll call you if it's not okay." Don jotted Hank's address on a memo pad.

"I'll be there," Cory said. They finished their light breakfast and left her house together.

"Did you lock your front door?" Don asked.

Cory appreciated his concern. "Yes, thanks," she said, as she hurried toward her office.

Odd neighbors were one thing, but Goldie's reports of a woman's cries should demand attention. Cory felt she might well have been remiss in not acquiescing to Don's suggestion. She looked forward to the meeting and hoped to redeem herself.

* * *

At seven minutes to eight, Cory left home in ample time for the short walk to Hank's house for the eight o'clock meeting.

She arrived a few minutes early.

Goldie answered the door and greeted her with a hug.

Tall, slender in tight black jeans, emphasizing her youthful shape, she wore an aquamarine silk shirt the color of her eyes. Her long white hair was braided into a ponytail.

"Hello dear. I've heard so much about you from Don. He's quite taken with our celebrity neighbor."

"He's also quite taken with you, Goldie. He praises your many attributes."

"Don is quite a guy—big on praises, and rarely complains," Goldie replied.

She escorted Cory into Hank's huge living room where over a dozen folding chairs formed a circle.

The group assembled around a large table displaying a stack of plates, napkins, and platters of cut fruit, cheese wedges, veggies, crackers, and cookies. Several empty gift bags for wine were scattered in the corner. Hank, the host poured wine.

Cory had expected a business meeting and was unprepared for a party. She hadn't brought any refreshments, and felt she had committed a faux pax. But it wasn't her fault. It was Don's, but she knew he was too kind to have deliberately embarrassed her.

After a reasonable time for chitchat, Goldie called the meeting to order.

"Everyone, I'd like you to meet Cory Cohen. It was her idea that brings us together. "We're all interested in what you have to say," Goldie said.

"I'm grateful to be here among concerned neighbors, and for the lovely refreshments on the table.

"Rita Rivers is my next-door neighbor. We've always informed each other whenever we expect to be away from home for a couple of days or more. Her car is in her garage and she was last seen jogging in our neighborhood.

"If she had left of her own accord, she would have asked me to feed her cat, and pick up her mail as she did whenever necessary.

"Rita did nothing of the sort with me or with her office staff. They are very worried about her. They told me that she has never before missed important engagements. Her disappearance is a fact. I reported it to a deputy sheriff. She notified Missing Persons. An investigator interviewed me and I provided all the information I had about Rita.

Now, I have reason to suspect our reclusive neighbor may be holding Rita captive."

A young woman screamed, "Oh my God!"

"Do you have any evidence?" asked a soft-spoken woman.

"So far, I don't think it's strong enough to have his door knocked down, but let's put a few clues together. Goldie, please share your observations."

"Because I suffer from insomnia, to tire myself, I stroll around the neighborhood for a half hour or so in the wee hours. A couple of days ago, I was out at three o'clock in the morning—still dark. A lamppost across the street from his house shone on his front door. I stood in the shadows and watched the recluse tiptoe out, look both ways before he rolled out his garbage containers for the weekly trash pick-up.

"Then he opened his mailbox, grabbed the contents, and tossed it into the recycle bin without first checking through it."

"Eccentric behavior, for sure," Cory said.

"There is more. While his door was open, I heard a woman crying inside his house. At first I thought it could be the TV, so I waited until he shut the front door behind him.

"I leaned my ear against his door and heard a woman cry and moan." Given Rita's disappearance while jogging in our neighborhood, I suspect she may be his victim," Goldie offered.

A tall middle-aged man sporting a crew cut stood. "My name is Bill. I may have the distinction of the only one here that spoke to him—although his response wasn't verbal or normal."

"I'll explain," he continued. "My backyard faces his. The first time I saw him, we were out weeding our gardens. I'm sure he hadn't noticed me, because when he looked up, I said, 'Hi' and I waved to him. He grimaced and ran inside. I thought it odd, but figured he had to answer his phone.

"About a month later, exactly the same scenario reoccurred. That was months ago. I think he's scared to come out. His garden is an eyesore. Is this the behavior of a normal person?"

"No, but it isn't evidence of a crime," Goldie said.

"True, but it's odd," Bill replied. "Now, early this morning as I was tracking a bird through my binoculars, I noticed the shadows of two human figures behind his drapes. It surprised me. I figured he's a loner."

"Bill's statement substantiates peculiar behavior, and Goldie's report casts a suspicion, but these incidents may not be enough for the authorities to burst through someone's door. Therefore, I suggest we patrol—twenty-four seven until substantial evidence is noted," said Cory.

"How much more evidence must we have?" A woman asked.

"Good question. If it were up to me, I'd say another cry or moan heard by more than one person." Cory said. "Maybe we'll be done tomorrow. I'm afraid, the longer we wait, the worse it can be for his victim, assuming there is one. Don't get me wrong. I believe Goldie, but I wonder if there is another explanation for the sounds she heard. Perhaps the recluse is taking care of a sick family member.

"I suggest we partner with one or two in the group. If possible everyone should patrol several times a day. We need to check his house as often as possible and note anything suspicious. Do you agree?" Cory asked.

The decision to patrol the area surrounding the recluse's house was unanimous. Most people in the group said they worked at home on their computers and could arrange as much time as the mission required. Rounds would start after the meeting and continue around the clock. Anything suspicious would be immediately reported to Goldie. She would phone 911 and Don.

Don's job was to phone neighbors after Goldie's alert. His key word was, "Now"—the invitation to assemble across the street from the suspect's house to await the first responders—emergency medical technicians, accompanied by the sheriff or police.

A petite young woman called out, "I'm Jennifer. I tried to recruit his next-door neighbors for our group, but they weren't interested."

"That's a shame," Don said. I'll call on them tomorrow morning to alert them and ask them if they've heard or seen anything unusual from his house. They could prove most helpful."

"I'm Paul," said a short, thin young man. I'm happy to partner with Jennifer. I'll volunteer to keep the timetable and record findings."

"One more suspicious finding may be all we need," Goldie said.

A tall, blonde, middle-aged woman sporting eyeglasses called out. "I'm Pam. I'm up late writing and I walk my dog in the evening. I can take the latest evening hour."

Cory watched as over a dozen people circulated to form partnerships and schedules.

After fifteen minutes, Paul clapped his hands. "Everyone please take a seat and let's finish so we can enjoy the refreshments. And let's applaud our hosts Hank and Goldie."

The hosts received a standing ovation.

It pleased Cory to be part of a mixed age group with a unified purpose. Too bad it had to take a crisis to make it happen.

"We're fortunate to have a fine group with many talents," Cory said. "Goldie is an attorney. Can you locate the name of the owner of his house?"

Goldie nodded. "I'll work on it tonight. Now let's review our plan. If on your patrol, you notice anything untoward, report it to me immediately—no matter the hour. I'll call 911, and Don. Don will call you and say, 'Now.'"

"Reporters of suspicious activity should assemble across the street from the recluse's house in case the sheriff wants your statement.

"Paul, call me when you have the patrol list," Goldie said.

Cory was exempt from the patrol during her working hours, but she offered to patrol that evening with Don after they helped Goldie clean up. Several people joined the cleanup team, and within fifteen minutes, the job was done.

Don escorted Cory to her house and waited while she replaced her shoes with sneakers. She grabbed a flashlight and a white sweatshirt from the hall closet.

On patrol, they chatted softly until nearing the suspect's house. At ten o'clock in the evening, a bright moon and stars helped light the path, but it was dark and quiet at the front and side windows of the recluse's house.

They quietly paced the block several times, turned the corner, and walked around the block. The rear windows were closed. They repeated the chore three times and before returning toward Cory's house.

"Well, maybe someone else will get lucky," Don said as he pecked her on the cheek. I'll wait here until I hear you lock the door."

"Thanks, Don for being a *mensch*."

"Oh, don't forget our lunch tomorrow—unless we find Rita before." Don said.

"As grandma would say, 'from your mouth, to God's ears'." Securing the latch, she heard Don's footsteps as he jogged away.

≈27≈

The ringing of the phone awoke Cory. Yawning, she picked it up. "Hello."

"Did I awake you?" asked Don. "It's eight o'clock already."

"It's good you did. I've lots to do before going to the office."

"How about postponing your to-do list and come for a walk on the beach and then I'll take you to breakfast? We can have lunch another day. I'm eager to see you."

"You're tempting me, Don Koppel. You're evil."

"Succumb, dear lass."

"Okay. I'll be ready in fifteen minutes, dear lad."

Mundane chores like marketing, gardening, and housework were low priorities. She preferred a beach walk with a pleasant companion.

They chatted as they walked, sharing highlights of their histories, drawing them closer.

"I divorced eons ago," Don said. "We were too young for marriage. Governed by our gonads, we didn't know each other well enough. If she hadn't gotten pregnant, I doubt we'd have married."

"It happens to many people," Cory said.

"I know, but unless you experience it, it's hard to imagine abandonment. Your world crumbles.

"My two sons were born one and a half years apart. She couldn't cope with them—with us. She ran away, leaving a note promising to send money. We never heard from her again. It's as if she never existed," Don explained.

"Wow! How difficult for you and your sons!"

Don nodded. "It made me stronger. It happened at the end of my first year in medical school. I gave up my scholarship and got a job as a science teacher with the New York City Board of Education. My boys were always my priority."

"I've heard inspiring stories like yours too often—usually from women. It's heartbreaking. How did the boys turn out?"

"Amazingly well. They lived my dream. Alex, the oldest, is an ophthalmologist in New York. I'm very proud of his work with Doctors Without Borders.

"Bob is a medical researcher in Scotland. Maybe one day he'll find the cure for cancer."

"It's remarkable that you managed their advanced education on a teacher's salary."

"They earned scholarships."

"Commendable. You did a fine job. Do they keep in touch?" Cory asked.

"Thanks to e-mail and Skype, we make contact at least once a month, more often when they have news of their accomplishments."

Cory felt a growing kinship with Don and felt ready to open up. "My husband was a cruel, insensitive man who abandoned our children. I regret not having divorced him earlier."

"We have a lot in common," Don said.

She nodded, but withheld further information, unsure if Don would keep it to himself. That trait would keep her at bay. Otherwise, if it weren't for Ben, she could imagine Don as a potential romantic partner.

Quickly, she realized it was a bad idea to have a romantic involvement with a neighbor. If it didn't work out, it would be uncomfortable.

Friendship would do nicely.

Cory flashed on the idea that Don and Betty could hit it off, but she wasn't sure if either of them were ready for a serious relationship. Perhaps they all could be good friends.

She wondered why Betty hadn't called about the spa date, and made a mental note to phone her as soon as possible.

Cupid was a role Cory enjoyed and a trait she had learned from Grandma. Given the opportunity to introduce like-minded single people, Grandma would spring into action. She called it a "mitzvah."

An insightful, sensitive woman, ahead of her time, Grandma made long-lasting matches for heterosexual and homosexual couples and refused their gifts. "Your happiness is a gift to me," was her mantra.

Don and Cory walked in silence for a few minutes.

"A quarter for your thoughts," Don said. "I raised the price due to inflation."

"Sorry, Don. I was momentarily distracted.

"If we suspect someone is at risk, based on the observations of a few respected neighbors, it should be enough to take action," Don said.

"I agree. Goldie heard sobs, and cries. They could be coming from a child. In that case, Child Protective Services could investigate. I'll take the initiative and make some calls from the office. We can't afford to wait."

After breakfast, Cory invited him to see where she hung out—her office, a short walk from the café.

"Very comfortable digs. I like the décor," he said.

He donned his glasses to peer at her credentials. "My, my, our neighbor is an impressive shrink."

"This neighborhood is well-populated with shrinks," she said.

"I value your profession, Cory. I consulted a psychologist after my wife left. He helped me do right with my sons."

"You seem very well-adjusted, Don."

"I manage. It helps to reach out to people."

"I'm glad you reached out to me. It's comforting to have you as my new friend."

"Believe me, I appreciate our friendship," Don said, extending his hand. "Put it here, dear friend."

They shook hands. "I'll leave you to make the calls." Don checked his watch and hurried out.

* * *

Cory reached Betty's cell phone and left a message.

A significant period of time elapsed since any contact had occurred between Cory and the detective handling Rita's disappearance. She was determined to reach that department, but first she phoned Rita's real estate office for any news.

A man answered, "Mike Morgan, here."

"Hi, Mike. I'm Cory Cohen, Rita's next-door neighbor. Do you have any news about her?"

"Sorry, we don't," he replied.

"Did a detective from Missing Persons come to your office?" Cory asked

"Hold on. I'll ask around."

Cory waited a few minutes. On the phone, she heard a door shut.

"No one here has spoken with Missing Persons," Mike said softly. "I'd like to help find her. She's been my mentor for six months and has helped me tremendously. Can we meet in your office to brainstorm?"

"I have some free time now. Do you need my address?"

"I'm a realtor. I'll find you," Mike said.

Within ten minutes, Mike arrived. An attractive, tall, sturdy young man with a ruddy complexion and an athletic build, he sported jeans, a tee shirt, and sneakers. He shook Cory's hand and greeted her with a smile befitting a toothpaste ad.

"Pardon my appearance. I'm not seeing any clients today."

"You look fine to me," she said.

"Rita insists that I dress up for clients. She's big on making a good impression."

"It works well for her," Cory said.

"As an example of Rita's generosity, she insisted on shopping with me for the right kind of wardrobe, and lent me the money. She told me not to worry, that she was confident I'd pay her back from my first big commission.

"I feel I owe her a lot, because she had faith in me. She's a generous and considerate person."

"I understand. Do you have any idea who'd want to harm her?" Cory asked.

"I'm not sure. I've given her disappearance a lot of thought. She has no life apart from real estate. She never speaks of friends or family—just the benefit run. Her heart is into helping disabled kids. Because I can't see any connection with the charity and her disappearance; I figured it must be work-related.

"So, I decided to examine her client notes—recent and going back a few years. One fairly recent prospective client, a Frenchman Yves Dubois stands out. He wanted Rita to broker a deal for a quick sale of his house and offered to pay a higher commission than customary. I attended the meeting at her office.

"Rita is a fine businesswoman. She likes to make money honestly, and it seemed obvious there had to be a catch."

Cory nodded.

"This guy claimed co-ownership of the house with his common-law wife, a famous artist living in Paris, who asked him to sell the property quickly so he could return to Paris as soon as possible. He insisted the home was paid for in cash and had no mortgage.

"Rita told him before she would do business, she required a preliminary title report from a title insurance company to document he and his wife were the owners. The report would reveal any mortgages or problems.

"In addition, she required certified documentation from his wife of her willingness to sell the property at a specified price.

"Rita explained that after she reviewed all the necessary documents including the deed to her satisfaction, she would inspect the house before drawing up a contract with him.

"He agreed to those terms, but when she asked him to supply the co-owner's notarized signature stating the requirements for the sale, he balked. He said he had deliberately offered a higher commission to avoid having to wait.

Rita was very patient. She politely explained the situation to him several different ways. Either the man had poor English comprehension, or he was a con-man."

"Or both," Cory said.

Mike shrugged. "He was livid, out of control. I was glad I was in her office at the time. When he raised his fist at her, I grabbed him before he could throw a punch and tossed him out the door."

"Wow! You could report this to law enforcement."

"One of the senior partners in our office overheard the ruckus. He advised me to forget it. He said that kind of publicity could tarnish our stellar reputation."

"But your priorities are different than his. And I prefer yours. Please keep in touch. You and I and our neighborhood watch group may be the only ones in Rita's corner."

"Okay. That does it. I'll make copies of her notes and hand them over to the gendarmes," Mike said on his way out.

* * *

Mike called the next day and asked to drop by. She figured he wanted to keep the conversation secure.

"What's up, Mike?"

"I did a little sleuthing on my own. Unfortunately, Rita's notes were sketchy, probably because the guy left in a huff and she wasn't interested in representing him. She keeps detailed notes on prospective clients—the people she expects to represent, but his guy wasn't one of them.

"All she had written was his name Yves Dubois. No address of the property. I did a web search but his name is popular—mostly among doctors. None of the photos of men named Yves Dubois resemble him. We've got nada for the police."

"It's disappointing. I have a question for you—another matter, but possibly related. I passed a house in this neighborhood with a FOR SALE BY OWNER sign. Would you be able to find out who owns it?"

"Sure, that's easy."

Cory scratched Ashley's home address on the back of a card and handed it to Mike.

"Thanks for coming by," she said.

* * *

Cory called the number for the Missing Person's investigator and was kept on hold an inordinate time.

She disconnected and called again, using her strongest tone. "This is Doctor Cory Cohen. No one should be placed on hold when there is an urgent matter. I must speak to an investigator immediately or I'll file a complaint. If any harm comes to the missing person, I will hold the department responsible!"

Wow! Talk about assertiveness, Cory felt proud to earn the title!

A soothing voice came on the line. "I'm Sal Verano, department chief. How can we help you, Doctor Cohen?"

"I'm Rita Rivers' next-door neighbor. I reported her disappearance a few weeks ago. She was last seen jogging in our neighborhood. Her car is in the garage and she hadn't followed her usual custom of notifying me, and her business associates of an intended absence.

"When I reported this, I may have misled your department. Initially, I suspected foul play by her former husband living in Arizona or Nevada.

"But now, Gladys Goldberg, on our neighborhood watch committee reports hearing a woman's sobs and cries emanating from the house of an eccentric, reclusive neighbor."

Cory provided Goldie's phone numbers and address, and the address of the reclusive neighbor. "In my opinion, Rita is in danger and this information requires immediate action."

Verano promised to get on the case immediately. He was conciliatory and apologetic, blaming a recent change of personnel.

Cory wondered what the private investigator was up to when she had approached Don. That incident didn't seem to have any relevance to the reclusive neighbor—if indeed Rita was his captive.

With few appointments on her calendar, Cory had time to think about the neighborhood watch group. It offered comfort, protection and closeness with neighbors, and she enjoyed a growing friendship with Don.

Even though Cory and Rita weren't close friends, they had a good neighborly history of helping each other. Now, she had Kitty as a constant reminder of Rita.

Kitty had bonded with Cory and made no effort to hang out near her old haunts, in fact Cory couldn't recall Kitty going anywhere but the kitchen, the litter-box and on or under Cory's bed or on her lap. The term "scaredy-cat" fit Kitty's personality.

Rita's office staff collected her mail and there was little else they could do, except wait—and worry.

The scenario of the eccentric, reclusive neighbor and Rita made sense. It was easy to understand how it could it have happened.

Cory imagined him peeking out from a corner of his window at Rita, a delectable dish, during her daily jogs in the neighborhood. Lusting after her, he captured and imprisoned her in his home. Chilled by the grim image of Rita as a sex-slave gave momentum for action.

She thought back to the private investigator and wondered who had hired her. What was the connection between the private investigator searching for Rita and Rita's disappearance?

⸗28⸗

Cory arrived at the office with ample time to check her email before Ashley's appointment. She had a hunch that she would hear from Ben in a disguised form, but first she'd call Betty. Again, Betty didn't answer. Cory became alarmed. Betty had showed enthusiasm for a spa date and promised to confirm a time, but hadn't. Cory left her a message: "Don't worry me, Betty. Please call a.s.a.p."

Quickly, she scrolled down a long list of email messages from her psychology listserv. Most referenced the American Psychiatric Association's proposed modification of the Diagnostic and Statistical Manual (DSM). The changes provoked disappointment and anger among mental health practitioners worldwide. Familiar with the credible complaints, she scrolled down the list, hoping to read an important personal message.

Although professional issues confronting psychologists were routinely discussed online, they were submitted in a general way with patient identities carefully concealed. Cory exercised caution in her online discussions, although she posted and received political messages, mostly to and from trusted friends and associates, and her children.

Suddenly she remembered that before Ben had left on his latest mission, for security purposes, they each had opened a new, supposedly "super-secure" email account using a different name and password.

They would use their old accounts to contact each other with unimportant stuff and write coded messages to each other on the new accounts. How could she have forgotten about it? She scolded herself for having forgotten about it.

She clicked on her new account. Voila! She found an email sent from *The Clock*. Although Big Ben and Cory were on different time zones, they were on the same wavelength. Now she would have to decipher the message:

Dear Ginger,

Please forgive me for not writing sooner. I'm swamped with work as our company is planning to open an office in your neck of the woods very soon.

Tell Otto and Ziggy to arrange a party at Robbie's Garden to celebrate my return. Dust off your fancy duds, Ginger, and put on your dancing shoes, and you and I will show our guests a thing or two.

Don't be surprised if I show up at your front door in a couple of weeks,

Hugs and kisses,

Your dancing partner, Fred

Cory's hunch paid off. Ben's message, dated two days ago, was easy to decipher:

The Clock referred to Big Ben in London, his current base.

The familiar names belonged to Joe and Roberta's German shepherd dogs, Otto and Ziggy. If Ben hadn't mentioned them, someone else in error could have sent the email to her. Robbie's garden probably was a code for Roberta's lovely garden.

But if the trouble with his boss had ended, why did he need to send a disguised message to her new account? Did it mean there could be residual problems—and he was still in danger, but wanted to alert her to his plan? She felt her body stiffen.

She replied to the message:

Dear Fred,

Congratulations on the good news. A garden party to welcome you home sounds delightful.

Otto and Ziggy said they are thrilled to dress up for a change, and want to play bartenders.

The best caterer in town awaits the opportunity to execute her craft as a welcome home gift for you.

Hugs and kisses from your dancing partner,

Ginger

She read their letters several times and considered hers an appropriately disguised response. She wondered why he needed to write a coded message if his situation was fully resolved?

Perhaps Ben exercised caution and didn't want to chance the interception of his new e-mail address by his former boss.

Apart from Ben's email to her, the rest of the correspondence would be worthless to a spy—nothing but sales pitches.

The phone rang, distracting her from the computer screen.

"It's Ashley. Sorry I can't make our session. I may have the flu. The hotel-clerk sent up a thermometer and aspirin. I was going to call Doctor Green, but I assumed she wouldn't make house calls. The hotel has a doctor on call, and I'm guaranteed to be seen some time today."

"Sorry you're sick. I hope you feel better soon," Cory said.

Despite amnesia, Ashley remembered how to respond to emergencies. The brain is a magnificent organ. It blocked memory of a traumatic event but allowed memory of self-preservation tools.

Sometimes in an attempt to understand a patient, Cory imagined herself in that patient's shoes, and vice versa. She wondered how Ashley would have reacted were she targeted by a shooter. How would any normal human being respond? Many experience anxiety, and some develop a phobia. She had shrugged off the shooting incident. As the number of frightening incidents she experienced increased, her ability to handle them had also grown. Law enforcement personnel expect danger. Others rarely contemplate it.

Having no update on the shooting incident from the police, she assumed they had no information. No trail to follow, but she needed closure. Deputy Lowe's card was in her desk drawer stashed among a batch of cards in no reasonable order.

After shuffling through the disordered cards, she produced the one she wanted, and called Deputy Ann Lowe. After identifying herself, Cory asked for an update on the shooting incident.

"There wasn't much to go on," the deputy offered. "However, around the time the shooting occurred, there were reports of a notorious drug dealer observed in the neighborhood. Our sources say he was searching for a tall Asian woman, a rival, known in the region as the "Woman in Black." You matched her description. Perhaps your case was one of mistaken identity."

"Did the drug dealer catch her?" Cory asked.

"Maybe he thought scaring her was sufficient," said the deputy.

⸗29⸗

It was nearly noon and Cory hadn't heard from Don. She assumed the patrols were unfruitful.

She locked the office and strolled to the neighborhood café to meet him for lunch as planned.

Arriving before Don, she was directed to a comfortable booth. A few minutes later, Don rushed in.

Decked out in a dark blue sport shirt that matched his eyes, and a pair of pressed jeans and moccasins, he looked very handsome. A sudden wave of attraction struck her. Was it a result of Ben's prolonged absence, or the warmth of Don's friendship?

Don's engaging and caring manner touched her. Grandma would have described him as a "haymisha mensch," a Yiddish expression meaning a good person to whom one can easily connect. For Cory, it meant having a familiar, comfortable manner—as in the Brooklyn of her youth.

She wanted to compliment Don on how handsome he looked, but figured he'd think she was flirting. It wasn't the message she wanted to send.

"If authorities break into the house and find Rita, they'll probably need to notify the owners. It may facilitate matters. Has Goldie found information on the owners of the recluse's house?" Cory asked.

"We needn't worry about Goldie's efficiency. She'd win a prize for it. You only need to ask her once; and right away, she does the job. It turns out that the property is owned in a Family Trust. The executors are Anton and Jules De Angelo in Baltimore, Maryland. Goldie couldn't find any information on the De Angelo family, but if needed, she would contact the law firm that worked on the trust," Don replied.

"Goldie is a valuable player on our team," Cory said.

"You know, Cory, Goldie is the only person who reported hearing moans and cries from the recluse's house. Do you think she may have imagined it?"

"I doubt it, Don. If no one else heard the sobs after Goldie did, maybe Rita fell asleep or is in a coma, or worse—dead!"

"We've assumed the sobs came from Rita, but Goldie wanted to make sure of it; so at sunrise, she sneaked around the mishugina's house, and peered into his windows."

"Oh, my! Goldie sure has chutzpah—and excellent hearing. What would she do if he had caught her?" Cory asked

"She planned to pretend to be sleepwalking."

Visualizing the unusual scenario, Cory giggled.

Don produced a stern look. "This is not funny, Cory."

"I know it isn't, Don, but picturing Goldie's pretense made me laugh."

"I suppose it would be funny out of context. Anyway, one window on the side of the house was raised about an inch. Goldie peered in, couldn't see anything, but she distinctly heard a woman cry, "*¡Socorro! ¡Que alguién me ayude! ¡Ay, mi pobre hijo, Marcos!*"

"What?" Cory cried.

"As a former teacher in New York City, I understand every Puerto Rican cuss word, but this was too hard, so I wrote it down for someone to translate," Don said, handing her his note.

Cory shrieked, "Oh, my goodness. This proves the woman is Rita!"

"Calm down, Cory. How does it prove it?"

"Promise to keep a secret, Don?

"Of course," he said. "Tell me already!"

"I stumbled upon some information in her house that led me to believe Rita is Hispanic and has a mentally challenged son named "Marcos," Cory said softly."

"Go on," Don said.

Cory pulled out her cell phone. "I'm calling nine-one-one, while you call Goldie. I'll translate later. Tell her we have enough evidence that Rita is a captive at the recluse's house, and that I'm calling 9-1-1, now!"

Cory made the call and as they rushed out of the booth, toward the door, she cried out over her shoulder to the host, "We have an emergency!"

Jogging toward the recluse's house, they heard the siren from an approaching emergency vehicle.

* * *

Cory and Don arrived in time to see the neighborhood watch group, concerned expressions etched on their faces clustered across the street from the recluse's house.

Three official vehicles, doors ajar, were parked in the middle of the street in front of the house. The front door was wide open as an emergency medical crew entered, carting a gurney. A woman's screams subdued as she was carried out.

The scene nauseated Cory. At first she wasn't sure the woman was Rita, until she saw the long, thick jet black hair and matching brows—overgrown from lack of care, and heard her murmur, *"Pobrecito. Marcos, me dulce hijo. Ahora tu madre está segura. Te quiero mucho."* Cory translated: "Poor little Marcos, my sweet son. Now your mother is safe. I love you a lot."

"What Goldie heard earlier that alerted me, was Rita's cry in her native tongue for help. In her dire condition, her primary concern was for her son."

Cory's eyes filled with tears.

She dabbed her eyelids and approached a young medical tech. "I'm the victim's neighbor, Doctor Cohen, a psychologist working with crime victims. May I help?"

"Maybe later, after we attend to her medical needs," he said.

Cory joined her spellbound neighbors as they silently watched the uniformed officers leading the recluse toward their vehicle.

A repulsive sight in handcuffs, muttering, unkempt, shaggy beard and long hair, he wore a dirty, tattered tee shirt, khaki shorts, and flip-flops. As he passed by, she noticed his dirty overgrown toenails and his unpleasant odor.

It was hard to imagine Rita, the epitome of cleanliness and style in his repugnant company.

Cory stepped away from the group to take a deep cleansing breath.

Goldie joined her. The two women hugged.

"You're a hero, Goldie," Cory said.

"We all played a part in this horrible drama," Goldie replied.

"A drama with a good ending," Cory noted.

"Group hug," Jennifer said, her arms spread wide. They formed a circle around Goldie, hugging each other.

"What's going to happen to Rita?" Pam asked.

"She'll be taken to the emergency room for a full evaluation and medical treatment as needed. The Emergency Medical Technicians are the first responders. They arrive first with the necessary emergency equipment to monitor and safely transport victims," Cory said.

"But she's also psychologically traumatized. Cory, can't you help?" asked Pam.

"Gladly, but Rita may prefer another professional, one who doesn't know her. She's a good neighbor, but a very private person. I have to respect that."

Cory stepped away for a moment to phone Rita's real estate office to report she was found and is safe. To preserve Rita's privacy, she provided no details.

"What do you think they'll do with our weird neighbor?" John asked.

"He'll probably be booked and then taken to a County Mental Health Facility," Pam replied.

"He needs to be disinfected—sanitized. A long, hot, soapy shower and clean clothes," said Bill.

Cory suddenly noticed Don's absence. "Where's Don?"

"Don and Hank went to buy provisions for our celebration tonight," Goldie said. "Same place as our first meeting. Tonight at eight, everybody."

⸺30⸺

Betty usually responded to phone calls within the day received or the following day. Having made numerous unsuccessful calls to Betty's cell and home phones over the course of two days, Cory became worried and planned to notify the San Diego Police Department to investigate her best friend's disappearance.

Before going that route, she would give it one more try. She punched in Betty's home number and started to leave a message, "Betty, I'm worried about you and I'm coming over with the police..." A weak voice answered. Cory recognized it as coming from Betty's, hoarse throat. "Are you sick?" she asked.

"Yep."

"Can I help you?" Cory asked.

"Doc was here. Called in meds. Better tomorrow."

"Can I pick up your prescriptions, bring you food?" Cory asked.

"No. All delivered. Don't catch my bug. Stay away. Must sleep now."

"Who will take care of you, if not your best friend?" Cory asked, but Betty had disconnected, leaving Cory worried and sad.

Shortly after, her doorbell rang. She looked out the peephole and recognized the young man from the local florist.

She opened the door to his smiling face, as he handed her a lush bouquet.

Before she could tip him, he ran toward the van, calling over his shoulder, "Lot of deliveries in your neighborhood, and it's not even Mother's Day."

She waved, and read the card:

> Dear Cory,
> Thank you for being my friend and the best neighbor anyone could have. Kitty and I are very grateful. I expect to be home soon.
> Love,
> Rita

Cory smiled as she placed the fragrant bouquet into a large vase with water. The colorful flowers graced the dining table.

She figured Rita had ordered flowers for the members of the neighborhood watch group and wondered how she would have found out about the group. Perhaps she asked someone in her office to play detective. Realtors make it their business to know about neighborhoods.

Cory hoped to hear soon from Mike after he learned the names of the owner of Ashley's house. She also anxiously awaited a call from independent Betty. It would be wonderful if the medicine acted quickly and dear Betty would feel better.

At four o'clock, Cory heard a taxi pull up in front of the house. She peeked out the window and watched Rita walk to the door and ring the bell. She appeared much healthier than Cory had expected. Amazing what cosmetics and three days of hospital recuperation could do.

Cory opened the door, and embraced Rita. "It's wonderful to see you," Cory said.

Rita smiled. "And I'm so grateful to you for so much."

"Come in, please. We'll have some tea. Are you hungry? I can prepare a wholesome dish."

Rita shook her head. "No, I had a wholesome lunch before I was discharged from the hospital. Green tea is fine."

Kitty flew into the room and leaped into Rita's lap.

"You haven't forgotten me, have you, Kitty?" Rita said, stroking the cat.

From across the room, Cory heard Kitty purring.

"She's very smart," Cory said. "A delightful guest."

"I had hoped she was staying with you. We're very grateful."

"It was my pleasure. It's good to have you back, Rita," Cory said as she readied a tea-tray.

"While I was in the hospital, I had time to think about my life and the importance of good friends and neighbors.

I realized I've operated on a superficial level with people. This is how I thought I had to behave in my work."

"When people experience a crisis, they often evaluate their life, and start to make wiser choices," Cory said.

Rita nodded. "I had a chance to speak to a crisis specialist—someone like you. She was very helpful. She knew how I was saved from that depraved man. It made me realize the importance of friends and neighbors. You're a psychologist, I should have trusted you, of all people, and taken you into my confidence."

"The prerequisite of friendship shouldn't depend on academic credentials, Rita."

"Yes, but my point is, I was afraid to trust anyone—even you! Now, there are a few things about me, I want you to know. I was ashamed and afraid there would be gossip and a loss of community respect if I had revealed it."

"I appreciate your taking me into your confidence now, Rita."

"I have a son, Mark. He's also called Marcos, named after his dear father. He's a lovely boy, sweet, handsome, affectionate, but he's mentally challenged. Because I wanted the best for him, I checked all the schools that would accept him and teach him survival skills in ways I couldn't. I was willing to work two jobs to pay the tuition.

"But my husband Marcos, a good man, a hard worker, but not ambitious—content to be a manual laborer, well he was dead set on keeping Mark at home. He objected to my wanting to make something of myself, to my studies, to move past the lifestyle of my parents and sisters—and everyone I had known.

"None of my family understood me and my desire to place Mark in a special school to meet his needs."

Rita sipped the tea, her pinkie finger in the air. "My persistence paid off."

"I left Marcos, changed my identity, and met my goals."

"You're a remarkable woman, Rita."

"Marcos and I love each other deeply, and are devoted to our son. Marcos sees him often and reports to me every Sunday when I call him. He was worried when he hadn't heard from me. Imagine his relief when I called him from the hospital."

"Did you tell him what happened to you?" Cory asked.

"We usually don't keep secrets, but I was afraid he'd come here and kill that ugly man—even though Marcos is normally a gentle person. I told him I had an accident, and I'm fine, now.

"Marcos was so worried about me, that he borrowed money and hired a woman who had once worked for a private investigator to find me. Obviously she was unsuccessful."

"Not entirely; she interviewed Don Koppel, one of our neighbors, and it resulted in the creation of the neighborhood watch group. It was Goldie—Gladys Goldberg, who heard you cry out."

Rita smiled. "Flowers aren't enough to show my appreciation."

"Your disappearance has made us more vigilant. We've decided to keep the neighborhood watch group going."

"With me onboard, too, I hope."

Cory nodded. "You have another ally. Mike Morgan. He'll be relieved to hear from you."

Rita's face paled. "How did this come about?" she asked, a tone of suspicion surfaced.

"I called your office frequently to find out if they had any news from you. One time, Mike picked up the phone. He asked if he could come to my office to brainstorm.

"At our meeting, he told me about a prospective client, Yves Dubois—a man who nearly threw a punch at you. He considered him as possibly involved in your disappearance. He thought that wild, angry man could have harmed you, but he couldn't find his address in your notes or on the web."

"Oh," she said, breathing sighs of relief. "That nasty Frenchman was totally irrelevant. I wouldn't waste my time jotting down his address.

"You know Cory, you and Mike are the only people I would like to consider as friends. It was a pleasure to see Mike grow. I knew he'd be successful with a *little* help," Rita said.

* * *

Soon after Rita left, Betty phoned. "I'm feeling so much better. I'm returning to work tomorrow, and ready for that spa next weekend. How about you?"

"Happy you're better, Betty. There is so much going on in my neighborhood right now, I have to put the spa date on hold. I'll call you tomorrow when I have more information," Cory said.

"That's okay. In my down time, I considered your thoughts on the blackmailer. Like you said, he or she may not be motivated by greed. Perhaps the motive is to make his victims squirm as retribution for some imagined rejection. Since three psychologists, all with masculine first names, were targeted, possibly the blackmailer has sexual problems."

"An 'N' of *three* is not sufficient to jump to this conclusion—still you may be right," Cory said.

"Well, it gave me pause during my feverish state," Betty said.

"I'm pleased you're better, now. Hopefully, we'll go to the spa soon."

Right after she signed off, Goldie phoned to plan a party at Hank's house on Sunday to welcome Rita back. "Let's find out if she's ready for it," Cory said, and Goldie agreed.

She called again a few minutes later. "The party has to be postponed because Rita can't make it. Although not completely recovered from her ordeal, she's planned to fly to Las Vegas on Sunday to visit her family. The neighborhood watch group decided to meet informally anyway—no festivities, just a group of neighbors cherishing community spirit."

Since Rita's return to the neighborhood, Cory's phone rang more than usual. Many neighbors simply wanted to chat. She wasn't used to the volume of calls and the frequent interruptions, but along with the annoyance came the warmth and comfort.

After the third call early Saturday morning, she was tempted to ignore the next call; but upon hearing Mike's voice, she snatched the phone.

"Hi, Cory, I have the information you requested."

"Thanks, Mike. What have you found?"

"On my way to the office, I walked around that house. It seems to be unoccupied and in dire need of grooming. The listed owner is Madeline Michel."

"Madeline Michel? A familiar name, but I can't place it," Cory said.

"Could be she's the wife or common-law wife of Yves DuBois. They both have French names," Mike suggested.

"Very interesting," Cory said. "Last time I passed by the house, I saw a sign stating it was for sale by the owner. Wouldn't such a sale require someone informed about real estate? Do you know if anyone is representing the seller of that house?"

"As a matter of fact, I do. Rafael Jones. He's from a well-connected family. His parents are real estate moguls. Raffy's not a legitimate agent. He's a shady character. Known to frequent the local bars and the track. A consummate gambler, he'd bet his firstborn for a chance at big bucks. Probably holds a record for the number of times he's been tossed out of bars for disorderly conduct. The miscreant who tried to hire Rita must be Rafael's bar buddy."

"Thanks for the info," Cory said.

"How's Rita? Mike asked.

"She's doing remarkably well. A bit too thin now as expected from her ordeal, but she's still gorgeous."

"I'd like to see her. When do you think she'd be ready for my visit?"

"She's not here now. She went to visit her family."

"Oh, I never knew she had kinfolk. She never talks about them," Mike said.

"Yes, I know. She was a very private person, but I think experiencing such a horrible ordeal and being saved by neighbors has changed her. I'm fairly certain she'll want to see you when she's back home."

"Good. I have a question for you. Do you think it would be okay when she's fully recuperated—of course—for our firm to have a welcome home reception for her?"

"Mike, you probably didn't know Rita when the market thrived. Every time she made a big sale, she'd invite me to a gala reception with her colleagues. Very snazzy."

"Good information. Thanks, Cory."

"My pleasure, Mike."

≈31≈

Cory remembered her promise to call Betty to plan a date for the spa. She figured Betty would forgive her delay, as it had become a bad but forgivable habit to forget a promise when events spun either of them in different directions.

Betty answered the call, "I forgive you. What's up?"

Cory related the neighborhood news.

"Your life is never dull even in laid back Del Mar. I'm glad it all turned out well. So when are we doing the spa thing?"

"Is next Sunday good for you?" Cory asked.

They agreed to leave at eight in the morning. Betty would pick her up and drive there and Cory would drive back.

Cory sighed in delightful anticipation.

Early Sunday morning coastal fog made for poor visibility, but the jolly TV weatherman reported better conditions a few miles east of the coast.

Betty arrived at eight, carrying two steaming cartons of coffee and a bag of bagels. The two friends sat at the kitchen booth, noshing, sipping, and glimpsing out the window while waiting for the fog to lift.

Cory filled her in on the neighborhood events.

"I'm glad you have a good neighborhood. A person could croak in my building and no one would know until the scent became overwhelming. It's nothing like back home in New York where people genuinely care about one another. I recall when we had a blackout. I lived on the twenty-third floor. Neighbors carried water, candles, and chairs to the landings."

Cory nodded. "We had a sense of community there. It's where we grew up. Here, most people were raised elsewhere. I think many people would prefer to feel close with neighbors, but it may take a shared problem for it to happen. I'd like you to meet my neighbors—now new friends—especially this guy Don Koppel. He's divorced, a retired science teacher, raised two sons on his own, and he's quite handsome and fit."

"With that resume, I'd be delighted to meet him," Betty smiled.

"You will—first chance I get." Cory said.

A little while later, the two friends were on their way to the spa. In two hours, the sun shone brightly as they arrived at the ornate gate. Two security officers asked for their identification and passes to the facility. The guards admitted them without further ado.

The women gasped at the gorgeous grounds—flowers of every color and shape imaginable. Beautiful sculpture adorned the landscape.

"A visual treat," Cory said.

"Apparently, Bruce thought you're worth it. If we really like it, we may think we're worth it, too, and we'll do it again," Betty said.

"First we'll check prices," Cory answered.

Arriving at the reception center, they were welcomed by an attractive woman wearing exercise clothes that looked as if they were painted on her body. Jessica was their guide for the day. She ushered them through the dressing rooms, showers, Jacuzzis, pools, exercise rooms, and beauty treatment facilities.

An abundance of robust plants housed in colorful ceramic pots added charm and oxygen to the facilities.

Cory and Betty marveled at the state-of-the-art equipment, the likes of which were new to them.

Jessica explained that Sundays were usually quiet in the gym area. "Many guests reside on the premises for a week and check out on Sunday. Lunch, however, draws a crowd of regulars who live nearby. They come to enjoy the homegrown organic vegetarian meal in what you will find—a spectacular dining area overlooking the gardens."

Betty and Cory agreed to exercise first, shower, have massages before lunch, followed by pedicure, manicure, and facial.

"Just pick up any phone and ask for me when you're ready and I'll escort you to the dining room. Lunch is served until three," Jessica said.

After finishing their morning program, Cory called Jessica.

The dining room had booths that would seat people in fours or eights.

Jessica asked if they would mind sharing a booth with another couple. They nodded affirmatively and were brought to a booth where two men were already seated.

"Fancy meeting you here," she said to Bruce. He introduced Kurt and she introduced Betty.

"Bruce is a colleague, Betty. He's responsible for our fabulous visit here."

"I figured that out. This place earns the title of one of the world's best spas," Betty said.

"It's a great place to shoptalk. The booths are cushioned and private," Kurt remarked.

Cory nodded. "I've told Betty about the blackmail threats. She's a forensic psychologist."

"So am I," Kurt said, holding his hand out. "Put it here, pal."

Betty smiled as they shook hands.

"Another psychologist emailed me that he was also threatened," said Cory

"Was it Scott Drew in Beverly Hills? We play handball with him. He's informed us," said Kurt.

"Did he tell you the name the blackmailer used?" Betty asked

"Yes. Lee Thomas, another ambiguous gender name," replied Bruce.

"With interchangeable first and last names," said Kurt. I caught that too."

"So far there are three southern California psychologists with masculine names victimized by a blackmailer using a specific kind of alias. Tentative diagnosis anyone?" Bruce asked.

"The blackmailer has a sexual identity problem and was evaluated by a psychologist to determine eligibility for transgender surgery, but denied based on a diagnosis indicating serious mental problems. Now, the blackmailer is hell-bent on making psychologists suffer," Betty said.

Kurt piped in. "Good call, Betty. I agree, it's retribution; but I'm puzzled about why he targeted Cory, Bruce, and Scott—psychologists who do not provide psychological evaluations when there are psychologists specializing in evaluations, like Betty and me. As far as I know, no forensic psychologist has reported a blackmail threat. We're the most vulnerable to retribution from disgruntled patients."

"Interesting point," Cory said.

"You know, guys, Cory considered notifying the postal inspector of the blackmail scheme. Before more damage is done, that may be a good move," Betty suggested

Bruce nodded his head toward Cory. "Because of your sage advice, dear lady, my office is now as orderly and clean as a surgical suite. Heidi Smart is an incredibly competent manager. With your permission, she'll take care of the matter with the postal inspector," Bruce offered.

"Fine with me. You're very generous and I'm most appreciative," replied Cory.

"My pleasure. Psychologists enjoy helping others. It's our *raison d'etre*," Bruce said.

"I don't know that we'll solve the blackmail mystery, but some good has come from it—we've made a couple of new friends!" Cory said.

Everyone nodded. Kurt held up his water glass. "Let's drink to that," he said.

The waiter placed a large tray on to the table. "A variety of dishes to sample. We have plenty more of whatever suits your fancy."

Lunch turned out to be an epicurean delight and they refilled their plates several times.

"Thanks for the memorable feast. The lovely setting and fine companionship," Cory said.

"Let's do it again," Kurt said.

"We'll celebrate the capture of the blackmailer," Betty said.

"Hope it won't take too long. I enjoyed meeting you," Kurt said.

On the way home, reviewing their pleasurable day, Betty remarked, "They're a couple."

"Maybe the same way you and I are. It makes no difference, either way. We're colleagues and we can be friends, too," Cory said.

"But they probably live like royalty and we don't," nodded Betty.

"Wealth isn't a sin, if it's earned honestly, and it shouldn't be a detriment to friendship. Joe and Roberta are as precious to me as you are. We spend very little when we're together. We're happy for the companionship."

"Yes, but Joe and Roberta are down to earth. They don't flaunt their money. You knew Joe when he was a poor grad student. But unlike us, Kurt and Bruce have a lavish lifestyle. They seem to be very used to it," Betty said.

"True, but once in a while, we could splurge," Cory said.

Betty smiled. "I see a little role-reversal here. You're usually more resistant to expensive purchases than I am."

"I'm convinced that we can afford to celebrate our respective birthdays in a sumptuous setting. It's good for our physical and mental health."

* * *

A few days later, Cory heard from Heidi Smart, Bruce's office manager. "I've contacted the postal inspector and he's opened a case for us. I'll fax the release authorizing me to act on your behalf regarding the blackmail threat. So, it's three documents, I'll need from you. Sign the release and mail it back to me along with the blackmail letter and its envelope. Any questions?"

"None. I'll make copies and send the originals to you by certified mail from the post office today. I appreciate your efficiency," Cory replied.

"It's my job, but thanks for the compliment. Now, for your information, after Bruce put the word out, another psychologist has added his name to the list of threatened psychologists. Makes a total of four that have come to our attention so far."

Cory thought it could be just a coincidence that four psychologists with masculine names were blackmail targets when there were a high number of females in the profession. Unless the number of targets rose, four was of little statistical significance.

Cory thanked Heidi Smart—she with an appropriate name.

After posting the material, she heaved a sigh of relief, and hurried back to the office.

Fifteen minutes later, Ashley called, sounding chipper.

"I'm feeling much better. The doctor said I had a virus, and the best medicine was bed rest and extra fluids. The staff was very accommodating. They treated me like a princess. I'm completely recovered now. Germ-free. When can you see me?"

They made a two-o'clock appointment for that day.

As usual, Ashley wore carefully chosen clothes as one may expect from a sophisticated San Franciscan. Clad in casual khaki slacks, a long-sleeve tweed cotton sweater, brown leather walking shoes, and a matching purse, Ashley's fresh, young face was pale, devoid of makeup, apart from a thin line of rose color lip gloss.

Cory grinned. "Welcome back, Ashley. It's always a pleasure to see how well you put yourself together, but then again, you're an artist."

"Thank you. I realize this is a beach community and my style doesn't fit in, but I just don't feel right wearing shorts, a T-shirt, and flip-flops. I really feel I belong in San Francisco, or Paris."

"Sure, you're a cosmopolitan." Cory wondered what had brought Ashley to Del Mar but she wouldn't find out until the young woman's memory was restored.

"I usually don't discuss with my patients places I've visited, but I have a hunch this place may trigger your memory because it is remarkably outstanding," Cory said.

"Oh, please do tell me about it," Ashley said.

"It's a world famous spa, called "Palliative Spa." It's a precious gem placed in a gorgeous setting—an incredibly beautiful landscape with state-of-the-art gym equipment.

The dining room features healthful, tasty food that looks like a work of art and too beautiful to eat. Does this conjure up any memories for you?"

Ashley paused, wrinkling her brow in an effort at imagining the place. She shook her head. "Sorry, I can't recall any place like it, but it sounds glorious. Anyway, I'm glad you could see me so quickly. I must be quite a challenge to you—as I am to myself with this huge gap in my memory."

"In here, challenge is par for the course, Ashley."

"I felt we were on to something when you stopped the hypnosis session, Cory. I'm afraid I'll go mad unless I regain my memory. I wish you had another tool to pry it out."

"I understand how you feel Ashley. You're absolutely correct. We were on to something that seemed to frighten you. I wanted to be sure you were ready to handle whatever memories could surface. You know I'm here to support you."

"Yes. I'm ready right now. Can we start?"

Cory nodded and began the hypnosis session. Ashley responded quickly.

Cory replayed the hotel scene.

In vivid detail, Ashley revisited the hotel table where she sat with a companion overlooking the ocean.

Ashley's face was radiant. "This is one of the best days we've ever had. I'll always remember this setting, the food, and the weather. Everything is so vivid and perfect."

"Who is with you?" Cory asked.

Ashley's face turned ashen. She bowed her head. Cory thought the young woman was about to faint.

"How do you feel? Would you like a drink of water?" Cory asked.

Ashley rose from the chair, "I can't go on. It's unreal. A nightmare. No! No!" She screeched.

"Why are you frightened?" Cory dashed to Ashley's side, ready to catch her if she fainted.

"It can't be. No! No!" Ashley's hands flew up to cover her face.

Clearly, Ashley's revisiting the scene was highly traumatic.

Cory guided her into the chair. "Ashley, please sit. We'll change the scene and go back to a safe, pleasant time in your early life. Can you remember your first friend?"

Ashley sat, closed her eyes, and breathed slowly and deeply for a few minutes as instructed. "Oh, goodie," she said clapping her hands. "Marie is my very best friend." Ashley's face took on the glow of a child.

"Where are you and Marie?"

"We're in a big, big garden with lots and lots of fruit trees. We're filling our buckets with figs. Gigi promised to make something sweet and tasty for us. We're counting the figs in our buckets to see who has the most. Oops, my bucket falls. Figs spill out. Marie helps me gather the figs from the ground. Our pails are full. We skip into the kitchen without dropping a single fig. We give our buckets to Gigi. She scoops ice cream and chocolate syrup she made herself into the biggest cups for us. We sit at the table and eat. Yum! Yummy!"

"How old are you?"

"We're five, maybe six."

"Let's go to a time when you're teenagers. Are you still friends?"

Ashley shook her head. "I missed Marie so much. We both cried when she went away to school."

"Have you seen Marie since then?"

"No," she said in the voice of a child, tears rolling down her cheeks.

"What do you remember after that?"

"Boarding school. I must have been six or seven. I missed Mama so much."

"How often did you see Mama?"

"Not enough, but I wasn't there more than a year or so. It seemed like more. I learned to paint there and I got good grades in French and English," she said proudly in a childish voice.

"Where was the school?"

"Outside of Paris."

"Where were you born?"

"New York City. In Manhattan."

"Do you have any sisters or brothers?"

"No."

"Tell me about your father."

"I never knew him. He died before I was born. Mama told me that he was a kind, loving, intelligent man."

"Describe your mother."

Perspiration formed on Ashley's brow. Her eyes glazed. "Mommy, oh, mommy," she howled.

"Why are you crying, Ashley?"

"I want mommy." Ashley sucked her thumb and rocked back and forth.

Ashley's regression surprised Cory. She considered her options. She could slowly bring Ashley back to the present, or continue the path from her childhood to adolescence.

It is natural for an only child without a father to have a strong bond with her mother. Cory wondered if something traumatic occurred to her mother in Ashley's childhood.

Cory recalled Ashley's earlier hypnosis session and figured a revisit to it could be fruitful.

"Let's move forward to the last time you had lunch at the Ritz Carlton Hotel. Describe the scene."

"It's a perfect day with a cloudless blue sky, bright sun. The weather is warm, like I prefer. In fact, nothing could be better, including the handsome, friendly waiter, around my age. The tableware and furnishings are as elegant as the food."

"Are you dining with a companion?"

"Yes."

"Describe your lunch companion," Cory said softly.

"She's my beautiful, wonderful Mama," Ashley whispered.

"What is her name?"

"Mama."

"What do other people call her?"

"Madeline Michel. I'm so proud of my Mama. She's a celebrated sculptor, and a well-known antique collector from Paris."

A chill of surprise visited Cory. Madeline Michel was the name of the woman Roberta had met at Christie's auction in New York.

No wonder the tapestry at the Inn had entranced Ashley. It was truly familiar to her.

And according to Mike Morgan, Madeline Michel owned the house. The house where Ashley awakened with amnesia!

"Where and when was the last time you saw Mama?" Cory asked.

Ashley became silent and Cory patiently waited.

The young woman trembled, eyes closed, she soldiered on. "I've come home earlier than expected from helping an elderly neighbor. I'm engrossed in an art book on Michelangelo in my room at the Del Mar cottage.

"I hear Yves cursing and screaming at Mama. That awful man is out of control. I open my bedroom door, ready to dash out to help her. His back is toward me, but I can see him leaning over her. His grubby hands are around her throat. Oh, my God, Yves is choking her—strangling her!" Ashley screamed. "He's killing Mama. She's not moving. Is Mama dead?"

Stunned, Cory realized Yves must be the vile man Mike Morgan tossed out of Rita's office.

Ashley, still hypnotized, continued to recall the horror.

"I start toward her. Monty stops me. He pulls me back into my room, whispers to me. "Don't let crazy Yves know you're here or he'll kill you, too!" Ashley shivered.

Picturing the scene, Cory's spine tingled. "Who is Yves?" she asked.

"Mama's beastly lover."

"Who is Monty?"

"He and Janusz are the men Yves and Mama trust to transport her antiques and sculptures."

"Is anyone else in the house?"

"Janusz is up in the attic."

"What does he do there?"

"He and Monty bunk there, but when they're out, I use a corner of it for a studio because of the skylight."

"Tell me about them."

"Jan's a big, burly Polish man with a huge gut. He doesn't speak English well, but he understands some. Monty is a Brit, about my age. Tall, lean, but strong like Janusz, only nicer and more sensible."

"Are they professional movers?"

"They're more than that. Yves treats them like they're his slaves. I don't understand why they put up with him."

"Where are they now?"

Ashley sobbed. "I can't imagine where they could be." Globs of perspiration peppered her face. Her cotton sweater clung to her chest and arms. "Maybe I fainted, or was knocked out. I don't know if Mama is alive," she screamed, tears gushing down her cheeks.

"What happened next," Cory whispered.

"I don't know. I don't remember anything until I awake in terror, not knowing where I am—or even who I am. I look around inside a strange house. Nothing looks familiar. I'm scared, terrified, confused. I don't know what to make of it."

The session was a breakthrough. It was a good time to stop.

Slowly and gently, Cory brought Ashley out of the hypnotic state. She told her she would remember the session and would receive the help she needed to process the trauma.

When Ashley opened her eyes, Cory was leaning over her, mopping the young woman's brow with a fresh, dampened hand towel.

"Thank you," Ashley whispered. "Now I know why I lost my memory. Mama was the most important person in my little world. It was just the two of us most of my life. We had no other family." Ashley wept.

Instinctively, Cory wanted to cradle the bereft young woman in her arms. She reached toward her, but Ashley stiffened, as though succumbing to Cory's gesture would be a betrayal of her mother.

Moments later, Ashley regained her composure.

"Now that I remember all of it, I must do the proper thing and notify the authorities."

Cory nodded. "Absolutely."

"I expect it will take time to come to terms with the brutality and my helplessness. Perhaps it will take my whole lifetime to mourn the loss of Mama."

"Time—not necessarily a lifetime—is the best healer. Most people having lost a loved one unexpectedly, experience a profound sense of loss. They had no time for preparation."

"I was blessed to be her daughter." Ashley dabbed the residue of tears from her cheeks.

"She must have loved you very much, and was proud of her fine, lovely, talented daughter."

"Yes. She told me so many times."

"It can be harder to grieve alone, Ashley. Do you have any family?"

Ashley shook her head. "It was just Mama and me during my childhood. My father died before I was born. My only connection to him is his name Anthony Hogan on my birth certificate and the generous inheritance he left Mama and me. She told me he had looked forward to my birth and would have been an excellent father. As far as I know, there are no other relatives."

"You probably have thoughts and feelings about that. It's a worthy subject for future discussion when you're ready," Cory said.

Ashley shook her head. "I don't think so. I've never missed having relatives. Early on, I understood from the few friends I had, how complicated it can be when one doesn't get along with a family member."

"True. But at a time like this, a grief group may be better than grieving alone. If you're interested, I can find such a group for you."

"No, not right now. Maybe later. I have way too much to digest. It's not just a murder—it's so much more. First thing I must do is to give the police a description of Yves. He should rot in hell!" she screeched.

"Yes, he should," Cory agreed.

It was natural and healthy for Ashley to unharness rage at her mother's killer. Cory handed her phone to Ashley. "Press 9-1-1. You'll reach the Encinitas Sheriff. Ask for Homicide. You've had a shocking breakthrough and it'd be better if you wait for them here. I'll stay with you."

"Don't you have other appointments today, Cory?"

"No. I want to be here in case you need me. Would you like iced tea?"

"Yes, please."

Cory stepped out of the office to brew chamomile tea and grab some ice cubes from the small refrigerator. Through the open door, she saw Ashley's face crunched in pain, her cheeks glossy from tears.

"Thank you, Cory," Ashley said between sips of tea.

About fifteen minutes later, two detectives in plainclothes arrived at Cory's office. Detective White, a short, stocky man with brown hair cropped in a crew cut, appeared to be around forty years old.

His partner, Detective Chavez, also short and stocky, with thick, black hair, appeared more mature, perhaps in his fifties. They showed their identification to the two women. Polite and ordinary looking—the kind of men that meld into the background. Perfect for detectives, but not at all like her man Ben. She invited them to use her office.

Cory wanted to digest the situation alone. "Are you comfortable with me leaving for about ten or fifteen minutes?"

"Yes," Ashley replied. "I feel safe here."

Cory walked briskly along the street to clear her head. When she returned, almost fifteen minutes later, the plainclothes detective's car was still parked in front of her office.

"We've been waiting here for you to answer some questions, Doctor Cohen," said Detective Chavez.

"Is that okay with you?" Cory asked Ashley.

"Of course. You're free to tell them everything you know about me." Ashley said.

"In your professional opinion, what's Ashley's diagnosis?" asked Detective White.

"It appeared to me, when I first met Ashley, that she had retrograde amnesia. I referred her for a complete physical and neurological examination that confirmed my diagnosis.

"This kind of amnesia is often the result of an emotional trauma, too frightening for immediate recollection.

"In Ashley's case, slowly, she began to recall some events in her past. It wasn't until today when we used hypnosis that she recalled the brutal murder of her mother."

"Could she have imagined it?"

"I don't believe so."

"Do you have any proof?" asked Detective White.

"I have Ashley's statements," Cory responded.

"Can't sick people make up stuff to gain attention?" Chavez asked.

"Yes, they can, but I have no reason to doubt Ashley."

"How long have you been in practice?" White asked.

"Several decades. Enough experience to make an appropriate diagnosis," Cory answered.

"Haven't patients ever lied to you?" Chavez asked.

Cory considered the grilling inappropriate, but let it go. "Some patients may stretch the truth, but when they present as Ashley has, I'm inclined to believe them."

"Maybe you don't recognize when patients lie," White smirked.

"Are you implying that Ashley may have fabricated amnesia to protect herself?"

"It is possible," Chavez said.

"I can't believe what I'm hearing," Ashley mumbled.

"Ashley and her mother were very close. There aren't any other family members," Cory said.

"That is what Ashley told you, doctor."

"Do you have information to the contrary, detectives?"

"No, not yet, but you may be too trusting, doctor," Chavez said in a condescending tone.

The detective's approach surprised and angered Cory.

"You're wasting precious time. If I were you, I'd rush to the crime scene with a forensic team and investigate the characters Ashley mentioned. Find out about her mother; who she is; where her body may be buried."

"You watch too many cop shows," White said.

Chavez laughed. "When did you become a detective, Doctor?"

Cory's annoyance grew. "Do you know Detective Lewis?"

"Never heard of him," White said.

"Nope," Chavez shook his head and chuckled. "Oh wait a minute. Isn't there a fictional English detective by that name on TV?"

"I don't appreciate your attempt at humor, detective. I suggest you check the 1999 case files of the San Diego coastal serial rapist. You'll find my name in your files. I worked with Detective Lewis to solve that crime."

"You gotta be kidding," Chavez laughed.

"I warned you about shrinks," White muttered.

Cory raised herself from her chair. Standing, she was taller than either of the detectives. She took a deep breath before raising her voice, "Stop wasting time and get out of here and solve this murder, or I'll do it for you. See how that, and your disrespectful manner, sits with your chief!"

"Don't threaten us, or…"

"Or what?" Cory placed her hands on her hips

Ashley's mouth dropped. "Oh, dear God!"

"Okay, we're leaving. Give us the address and your house key, young lady. We'll return it here when we're done," White said.

"Thanks for your time, doctor." Chavez's words dripped with sarcasm.

After they left, Ashley rushed over to Cory. Quite out of character, she hugged her. "I'm so proud of the way you handled those insolent fools. You're an incredible woman—like my mother." She broke down in tears, weeping on Cory's shoulder.

Cory felt a maternal tenderness toward her patient. She must use it wisely to help her heal, not to replace the lost mother.

⸗32⸗

After Ashley's breakthrough session and the astonishingly disappointing interview with the detectives, a combination of anger and weariness enveloped Cory.

She had expected professionalism, not ridicule. Her previous experiences with local law enforcement agencies were very positive. Officers were professional, respectful, and helpful. During her long career, she called upon them on several occasions to check on the security of depressed patients who had consistently kept their appointments, but failed to show up and couldn't be reached. The officers had responded swiftly, and in one case, saved the life of a comatose patient.

Now, she wondered if Detectives White and Chavez were for real. In haste, she hadn't scrutinized their identification. She called the non-emergency number of the Sheriff's Department, identified herself, and asked for Detective White or Chavez.

"They're in the field. Do you want a call back?" a woman asked.

"It isn't necessary. I just want to be certain that I have the right detectives. Both are short and stocky. White has a crew cut and looks about forty. Chavez, a bit older."

"That's about right."

Relieved, she thanked the woman and disconnected the call.

"Thanks for everything, Cory. I'm sorry I caused you to be mistreated by those idiot detectives."

"You're not responsible for their behavior, Ashley."

"I may have to cry myself to sleep, but I think it'll help. Right now, I'm drained. Can we talk more tomorrow?" Ashley asked.

After they made an appointment, Cory headed home. She craved a shower, a pizza, and a call from Ben.

Preoccupied with the events of her day, she arrived exhausted. She slid a frozen pizza into a slow oven, and relaxed in the shower.

Drying off, she set the table for one, clicked on a CD of Beethoven's Fifth Symphony, and prepared a salad.

After an intense day, she usually welcomed solitude, dining alone and listening to music; but tonight was different. She was exhausted from the session with Ashley, and upset over the remarks made by the disrespectful detectives.

She craved comfort and support from a trustworthy, understanding friend. After dinner, a phone call to Betty or Joe would do nicely.

After she finished her meal, the phone rang almost on cue and she grabbed it.

"Hi Cory. Don here. We're meeting at Hank's at eight for a bit of chitchat. Should I pick you up?"

"Oh, Don. I'm sorry. Normally, I'd love to join you, but I had a hard day at work and I'm beat. Please explain it to the group."

"Will do," Don said before disconnecting.

She called Betty. Her best friend answered on the first ring.

"Do you have time and energy to hear about my distressing day?" Cory asked.

"Go for it," Betty replied.

Cory described Ashley's breakthrough session.

"Wow, that's worthy of an article for The Hypnosis Journal," Betty said.

"Not so fast, Betty. The detectives' ridicule of me has caused me to doubt my ability. From their perspective as investigators, they have a valid point. You see, in criminal investigation, suspicion is critical until proof is found. In retrospect, perhaps I should have been suspicious of Ashley's amnesia and not accepted it as the truth."

"Come on, Cory. Why would she make it up?" Betty asked

"To have an alibi for murdering her mother."

"What on earth! I'd never have considered such an outrageous thing," Betty said.

"Unlike criminal investigators, we're not trained to suspect foul play by those seeking our help. We're disposed to believe their words until they display an obvious incorrect perception of a conversation or an event."

"Quite right, Cory. Patients have nothing to gain from falsifying tales about themselves and their lives to their therapists. We're trained to recognize unusual misperceptions as symptoms of a mental disorder—that's our province."

"In other words, Betty, you're saying my behavior was standard. But we're talking about most patients. Isn't it possible that Ashley deceived me and conjured up the tale of her amnesia to hide her role in the murder of her mother?"

"Could she have concealed the precious art to claim insurance? Wouldn't the body have to be discovered to process a claim? Maybe there wasn't any Monty, Janusz, or Yves. Such odd names could be inspired by a creative imagination. And Ashley is clever," Cory said.

"Those are questions the detectives are probably asking themselves. They shouldn't lay it on your lap."

"Apparently they wanted to raise my doubts about Ashley."

"Psychologists usually don't expect a patient to deliberately supply misinformation to create an alibi for a misdeed-or a serious crime," said Betty.

"In all my years of experience, I've never mistaken a patient's motives for seeking psychotherapy, Betty. If Ashley is a fraud, she's also a consummate actor. I'm inclined to trust her until evidence proves otherwise."

"Makes sense to me," Betty said.

"Wait a minute, Betty. I actually did become suspicious early on, when hypnosis wasn't working. I was ready to give up on her because she seemed unwilling to try."

"Yes, I recall you considered a diagnosis of dissociative personality disorder because she behaved uncharacteristically in that incident."

"Right. It was then that I suggested we terminate therapy and she asked for an alternative to help her find out more about herself. That's when I suggested she contact the local newspaper to publish a newsworthy article about her amnesia—some headline such as "Do you know this woman?" Or "Who Is She?" in the hope someone would come forth and fill in the details for her."

"What became of your suggestion?" Betty asked.

"Ashley said she was scared to do that and was unwilling to figure out her reasons. I thought it odd, but dismissed it when she called the next day for an appointment. I don't know if this is significant."

"What does your gut tell you, Cory?"

Cory paused in thought. "I'm still inclined to trust her."

"I would trust her, too. Those detectives were rough on you. I suspect one of them had a bad experience with a psychologist—probably during his divorce or child custody case, so he's taking it out on you."

Cory laughed. "You're probably right. You've made me feel better. How about we return to the expensive spa this weekend?"

"I'd rather stay close to home this weekend and work on some projects," Betty said.

"You'd prefer to clear your desk or clean the walls than spend time with me?" Cory blurted. Her sudden outburst had sprung from her feelings of vulnerability and rejection.

"You know me better than that, Cory. I had planned to take care of household chores, but it isn't urgent. I realize you need me now more than my chores do. Actually, I'd welcome a break for lunch and a Saturday matinee. Would that work for you?"

"Oh, Betty, I'm so sorry I jumped at you. Blame it on my reaction to those disbelieving rude detectives. I felt humiliated. You're a great friend and I shouldn't take you away from your plans."

"It's okay. We're there for each other and I'd go nuts in the house for the entire weekend. Let's read the reviews and discuss which film to see. Call me Saturday morning ten o'clock."

After signing off, Cory felt ashamed of attacking and manipulating Betty. It was uncharacteristic, impulsive, and sprung from uncharacteristic vulnerability. She felt fortunate to have such a kind, understanding friend.

≈33≈

Monty couldn't remember how long ago the dreadful events had occurred before he awakened in a hospital bed, his leg in a cast and his head bandaged. What had happened to him was, by far, the worst day in his life. Gradually, he began to put the pieces together, trying to make sense of it.

As a tourist in California, he had gambled and lost a chunk of money at the Del Mar Race Track. It was there that he had met Yves over drinks at the bar. When Yves asked him his line of work, he told him he hauled antiques for a collector. Yves said it was their lucky day as they could be helpful to each other. Yves offered him a job involving the transport of precious art objects. It paid well and included room and board. He would be able to save for a ticket home.

Soon he learned that Yves was a con man, and a horrid person. Had he known the man's propensity for violence, he'd never have gotten involved with him. Mum had always cautioned him to carefully choose his mates. He remembered her telling him, "You're too trusting a fellow, my boy." Mum was right as rain.

Now, he couldn't get the image of Yves strangling Madeline out of his mind. It haunted him. Yves hadn't shed a tear, nor expressed any regret for the woman he had professed to love.

Monty recalled the scene as if it were a horror movie he couldn't get out of his head.

Emotionless, Yves had shared his plan to dump Madeline's personal stuff into the large black plastic bags the gardener had stored in the shed.

He would wrap Madeline's body in a blanket and shove it and the bags into the large trunk of his leased Lincoln Town Car. He planned to drive along the coast and toss her stuff into a trash bin on the beach before dragging her body into the ocean.

Monty remembered Yves's words: "Luck is with me. The coast is so foggy, I won't be seen."

Monty figured Yves was not only a cold-blooded killer, but also a fool not to consider the danger of driving in thick fog.

Yves had handed him the keys to the storage facility and ordered him and Janusz to carefully pack and haul the entire art and antique collection from the house into the van. They were to move everything from the house and drive thirty miles to the storage facility. He warned them not to waste time. It had to be straight away.

Monty recalled having protested. He remembered telling Yves that driving thirty miles in the fog would take at least an hour and a half. Couldn't they wait until the fog lifted?

"No, no, no!" Yves had said. Monty pictured the scene, remembered Yves' eyes blazing, insisting they start the job right then.

They were to wait for further instructions from Yves outside the storage building. Monty regarded the task as difficult and dangerous. It wasn't worth the chunk of change Yves had promised, but without his promised earnings available, he had felt compelled to follow through.

Now, he recalled the sweat pouring down his face, blurring his vision and his struggle to see the road ahead, as he slowly hauled the van with its precious cargo through the fog.

Monty had worried about being pulled over by a suspicious patrol car. What if the cops decided to inspect the van's contents? What then? There weren't any papers to prove the cargo wasn't stolen. And stolen from a murdered woman, no less! They wouldn't be safe until the stuff was in storage. Even then, they could be in danger.

Spooked by Yves's unexpected rage, Monty had decided it was imperative to plan an escape from him. Too late for regrets. The hell with the money now, he remembered thinking. I'd sooner dig ditches or beg on the street. And if worse comes to worse, ring Mum and ask her for a ticket home.

He wondered then as he did now—about Madeline's sweet daughter Ashley and how she was coping. He wished he could have done more for her, but it was impossible without revealing her presence and placing her in danger from Yves or Janusz.

Monty had tried to console himself with the probable fact that she was safer inside her room, undetected by her mother's killer. Ashley was a lovely, sweet person. If circumstances had been different, perhaps they could be chums. She was always polite and treated him with respect. For a rich kid, she wasn't haughty. But then again, she was an American, wasn't she then?

Thank God, Yves hadn't realized Ashley was home and had witnessed his dastardly act. At least Mum would be proud of him for protecting an innocent young woman as best as he could under horrid conditions.

Monty recalled feeling trapped. He wanted to break away from Janusz, and to report the murder and theft to the police. Would they believe him? Would they protect him from retaliation by Yves and Janusz? If Ashley came with him, they would surely listen. Could he arrange that safely? He wondered what happened to her.

He had been afraid to ask for Janusz's help. Although they had shared living space, Janusz's lack of English comprehension kept them apart. Monty hated the lack of privacy and didn't enjoy the Polish man's company one iota. He was nothing like his mates in London, but at least he knew how to play a grand chess game—although in silence.

He recalled the fear and anxiety he had on that foggy night, his heart thumping hard, Janusz seated silently next to him. He had worried that if he had a heart attack, Janusz might dump him on the street to die. He had considered that Janusz might kill him to protect himself.

He needed to find out if Janusz had any loyalty to Yves, but it was useless. The damn man could not comprehend.

Monty tried to reconstruct their conversation word for word:

"Do you know Yves a long time?" He had asked.

"What you mean?" Janusz responded.

"I was wondering if you and Yves have a history," said Monty.

"*Heestry?* No understand." Janusz replied.

"When did you first meet Yves?" Monty asked.

"I no like talk about heem." Janusz said.

Monty was stymied. "Okay, I respect that."

Janusz shrugged his shoulders. Yves' violence may have also shocked Janusz, but it was hard to detect it. Monty was frustrated in his inability to communicate with his comrade.

Monty had never felt so alone, and so scared.

To distract himself then, as now, he imagined being back in London in the comfort of his usual pub with his mates, playing darts, downing malt ale, clowning around.

"Mum, I should have listened to you," he mumbled before he fell asleep.

≈34≈

Monty felt as if he were in a dream—or watching a film in which he is the lead character. He is parked outside the storage facility for over two and a half hours, weary, hungry and inpatient. Janusz is snoring softly.

Monty had made about thirty unsuccessful attempts to reach Yves on his mobile and had frequently checked local news on the radio and Internet for accident reports. There were some, but none matched Yves or his car.

Monty listened intently to an interview with a professor of oceanography from Scripps Institution. Asked whether fog and high waves could occur simultaneously, Doctor Flick explained that the combination creates hazardous conditions in Oceanside and Mission Bay Harbors. It was also more likely for large waves to occur in winter than summer.

Wow! That idiot Yves should have done a bit of research before taking off on his dangerous mission, he thought. But Yves was impulsive and not the sharpest tool in the shed.

Monty wondered what could be expected when dumping a body in the ocean. The interviewer must have read his mind.

> Question: What locations would the bodies likely surface?
> Answer: The path of a leaf dropping from a tree depends on the wind speed and direction at the time, and could go any direction. Similarly, bodies could go up or downcast.
> Question: Would the bodies likely surface together and at the same time?
> Answer: No. Almost certainly not. Two leaves dropped at the same time will not land at the same time and place. As part of our research into mixing and transport on beaches, we release "floating objects, each equipped with GPS" in a cluster.
> Question: How long would it reasonably take for the bodies to surface?

Answer: Bodies of local drowning victims have washed ashore in times ranging from hours to days to weeks to never.

In all probability, Yves had drowned and would not be mourned. Janusz would be angry because he had worked so hard for so little.

Monty feels a deep sense of relief. He would no longer have to deal with unpredictable Yves. He is glad that a murderer had gotten what he deserved.

He thinks of distraught Ashley. Longing to comfort her, he cautiously heads back toward Del Mar.

His eyes are burning, making it harder to drive in the fog, but his desire to help Ashley propels him on.

The bright lights from a large delivery truck roaring down the dark road heads toward the van.

⸗35⸗

Monty hears himself screaming. He is terrified. He wants to open his eyes, but he's too afraid of what horror awaits him. Suddenly, his eyes pop open.

A young man clad in green scrubs stands over him, trying to calm him. "It's okay. You're safe here in the hospital."

"What happened?"

"You had a traffic accident a few weeks ago, a head-on collision. You were taken here by ambulance and were in a coma until today."

"What are my injuries?"

"I'm not a doctor. I'm an aide. The doctor will be here in a few minutes. She'll explain everything. All I can tell you is what you can see for yourself. Your leg is in a cast. I reckon it's broken. You're lucky to be alive. The man in the passenger seat probably didn't know what hit him. Was he your friend?"

"No. He barely spoke English."

"I'll stay with you until the doctor arrives," the aide said.

"Meanwhile, I'll take your vital signs. Is there anything I can bring you? A drink of water? A newspaper?"

"Yes, thank you. I'd welcome both."

"I'll get them while the doc examines you," the young man said as he recorded Monty's temperature and blood pressure. He completed the task as the doctor strolled in.

"Hello Monty, I'm Doctor Hope," she said, smiling at him. "How do you feel?"

"I guess okay. I'm in a bit of a shock to find myself here."

"Of course. You're a very lucky young man. You were driving a van in the fog and apparently had a head on collision with a truck. There were many accidents that night. Most resulted in fatalities. You got off easy with a head injury and a broken leg. Sorry to say, your passenger was DOA. That means *dead on arrival*. What's his name?"

"I only know his first name, Janusz. We worked together for a short time and I didn't know him well. The bloke was from Poland and didn't speak English, so we couldn't very well be chums."

"I was told there wasn't any identification on him. His next of kin should be notified. If you're up to it, the police will want to speak with you later today," said Doctor Hope.

Monty had a lot to tell them, but first, he needed information.

"Would you happen to know if a man named Yves was among the fatalities?"

"I can't tell you that, but perhaps the police can," she said, placing her stethoscope on his chest.

"Heart sounds good. Now follow the light," she said, moving a thin-lighted instrument in front of his eyes.

"Although you seem to be in good shape, considering what happened to you, we must keep you here a little longer, just for observation and to make plans for your recuperation. Are you hungry, or thirsty?"

"Yes. A bit of both."

"We'll start you off with soft food for now, and please sip the water slowly."

"I'm very grateful to you for the good care."

* * *

Monty rested on the hospital bed. The aide brought him magazines, a newspaper, and a tray filled with a tall plastic goblet of cool water and a straw, a banana, and peanut butter crackers.

"Here you are. Your first-class dining order."

"Indeed it is right now." Monty smiled.

"If you want to watch TV, I can roll one in," the aide said.

"Is this a first-class hotel, or am I dreaming?" Monty asked.

The aide laughed. "Your condition warrants good service, Monty."

"I see your badge says you're Sam."

"Short for Samson, but there is no Delilah in my life."

Monty laughed. It felt good. He didn't remember laughing once since he had arrived in the states. "I'm single, too."

The two contemporaries chatted about single life, sports, and politics. It cheered Monty that Sam's views were much like his own.

179

Yanks weren't much different than Brits, after all. They did speak the same language—sort of, he thought.

"When I'm out of here, it would be nice to have a pint with you. I don't know anyone here. It was quite lonely with no one my age around and no time to make chums." And then he remembered Ashley.

"Sam, it's very important that I speak with the police about my accident. Any idea what time they'll arrive?"

"Can't help you with that. Today, I suppose."

Sam adjusted Monty's bed pillows and tried to make him comfortable.

Monty was grateful to Sam. Having someone to care for him now was especially touching after his grim life in the states. "Hospital care in the states must be expensive, Sam. I may not be able to afford it."

"Well, I don't know exactly how it works, but you're an accident victim and someone is financially liable."

"But who?" Monty grimaced.

"Don't worry about it now. The social worker here will help you when the time comes. I have to take care of other patients now, but I'll look in on you later. Sure you don't want the telly? Isn't that what you Brits call it?"

Monty nodded and smiled, grateful for the attention.

Sam rolled in the telly and handed the remote to Monty.

"Thanks mate!" Monty said.

⹋36⹌

Monty awakened from a nap and became aware of two men standing by his bed. They weren't hospital staff. They wore street clothes. One was tall and trim. The other was short and stout.

"Are you from the police?" Monty asked.

"Yes. I'm Lieutenant Bloom," said the tall one, "and my partner is Lieutenant Green."

"We're sorry to disturb you when you're resting. How are you feeling?" Green asked.

"Thank you. If it weren't for a broken leg, I'm right as rain. I'm glad you're here. I have much to tell you." Monty said.

"Routinely, we ask questions and you supply the answers." Bloom smiled.

"Fine with me."

They recorded the interview. When they finished, Monty asked, "Have you found Yves?"

"No, he hasn't turned up," Green said.

"And Madeline's body?"

"It hasn't surfaced," Bloom said. "You're sure she was dead?"

"I'm positive that she wasn't breathing when Yves wrapped her in a blanket before he went off to drown her body."

"He may have accomplished that," Green said.

Bodies don't always surface, and if it does, it may not be intact. Also, it may drift ashore miles away from where it drowned."

"We're very familiar with drowning situations in this area," Bloom added. "Bodies in the ocean may surface a long time after the drowning occurred."

"I'm certain Yves killed her. My concern is for her daughter Ashley Hogan. She has no family. I'm probably the closest person she knows here, although we really weren't chums. I worked for her mother and Yves. I'd like to know if she is safe."

The two men started to leave.

"Please wait. I believe I'm entitled to know about Ashley. We shared the same house and witnessed the killing of her dear mother right in front of us. Ashley is a tender young woman, all alone here."

"We understand your concern and we'll do what we can," said Green. "We'll be in touch with you as the case develops."

They started to leave the room, when Green's mobile phone rang and he picked up the call. He stood for a moment at the door and then came back and sat down on a chair near Monty's bed.

"I have some interesting news for you. I've just gotten a report from INTERPOL. I'll read it to you. Fingerprints of the recent auto accident victim in San Diego County, California match those on file for Janusz Gorski.

Gorski is listed as a member of an elite group of international investigators of stolen antiques, art, and artifacts. He is fluent in eight languages: Polish, Russian, Greek, Italian, French, Farsi, Arabic, and English. He is also an international chess champion. His most recent assignment was to the USA to track a priceless antique tapestry."

Monty's eyebrows rose. "What? This is unbelievable!" The Janusz I knew was illiterate, unable to speak English or French. Now, it turns out he's fluent in eight languages? Imagine that!

And to top that off, think I, an amateur chess player, played with an international champion? No wonder he always won!"

Green and Bloom smiled as they left the room.

⸗37⸗

A ringing phone awakened Cory. Her bedside clock displayed 8:05. Surprised to have overslept, she grabbed the phone, "Hello."

"Hi, Cory, it's Ashley. How soon can you see me?"

"Is it an emergency?" Cory asked.

"No. No. You sound groggy. Sorry if I woke you. I'll call you later."

"Really, it's okay, Ashley. I'm usually up by this time. I'll check my schedule. Hold on please." Cory grabbed her calendar. "I can be at the office by ten."

"See you then," Ashley said.

Cory hopped out of bed, realizing that she must have been exhausted to awaken over an hour later than usual. Coping with the aftermath of Ashley's trauma had sapped her of energy.

She started the coffee. While it brewed, she showered, toweled off, and dressed. Between gulps of coffee, she nibbled a nutrition bar and then headed for her office.

Cory hurried down the sidewalk. To her delight, all the Jacaranda trees in the neighborhood had bloomed overnight. Purple flowers atop the trees lined both sides of the street. The flowers wouldn't last long. Very soon they would carpet the ground. She glanced at her Timex. She had sufficient time to photograph the scene on her mobile. A thing of beauty should be shared.

As she approached her office building, she spied Ashley seated on a sidewalk bench, reading a newspaper. She appeared relaxed. Cory watched her for a few moments before approaching.

"Hi, Ashley. Seems we're both early for our appointment. Do you want to come in now?"

"Oh, I was so engrossed in this newspaper article, I didn't notice you. I'll tell you about it inside. Let's go." They walked together into the office.

"After the detectives were so rude to us, I never thought I'd get anything good from them, but they called at seven this morning and met me at the Inn. Surprisingly, they were actually very polite—I guess you'd say 'conciliatory.' They told me Monty had an automobile accident and was recuperating in the hospital and has asked to see me. I had to call you early to tell you. I'm going to visit him after this appointment."

"Well, that is truly good news!" Cory smiled.

"He saved my life. Now, I must take care of him."

"That's terrific, Ashley. It'll be good for both of you."

"I've thought it all out. It would be best to stay in adjoining rooms at the inn for now. We'll have each other's company. He's a very sweet guy. We can be a comfort to each other."

"I'm happy for you. What's his medical condition?"

"The detectives couldn't tell me because of health confidentiality laws, but Monty will explain it. I don't know how long he'll be hospitalized."

"Whatever it is, I have confidence that you'll cope well with it," Cory said with conviction.

"Oh, I almost forgot the really big news in the paper.

Yves's rental car was found abandoned near the beach in Cardiff. Investigators sent his fingerprints to an international database and learned he is an international antique thief wanted in France. Authorities here suspect he drowned, but the likelihood of his body surfacing anywhere or anytime soon is uncertain."

"Oh, my goodness!" Cory exclaimed.

"I think this situation with Monty will turn out well for both of us," Ashley continued. "He'll have someone to take care of him and I'll have his company."

"Survivors can support each other," Cory offered.

"Monty has been through a lot. He may need you for therapy, Cory. I want to pay for it. I have money and he doesn't."

"Ashley, when one friend has a lot of money and the other has none, it can become a problem for them. At some point, it will be important to deal with this issue with Monty. He may dislike feeling dependent and come to resent you for it."

"Oh, I didn't realize that. I'm glad you told me. It certainly wasn't the case with Yves and Mama. I know he didn't love her. If he did, he would have treated her nicely—not killed her. He would have treated me nicely, too, not been jealous of me."

"It sounds like you've made an accurate assessment, Ashley. You and your Mama were very close, especially since there were no other relatives. Yves couldn't possibly dismantle a tight mother-daughter bond."

Ashley nodded. "I was always certain Mama would never abandon me for any reason. I knew early on that Yves loved her money and her prestige. He thought it would rub off on him. Make him look better. He liked to show her off because she was beautiful and talented and rich. No, he wasn't resentful of her wealth at all. In fact, I think he clung to her because of it. He never acted kindly toward her, and certainly not to me. I begged Mama to leave him because he scared me and I was afraid for her, too. He often told me I was jealous of him. I suppose I was jealous of the time he stole her away from me."

"You know, Cory, I've never hated anyone except for Yves, but I never expected him to kill her. If he wanted to kill anyone, it would be me. He was jealous of her love for me."

"I don't know Monty, but I'd bet he's nothing like Yves," Cory said.

"I'm sure at some point Monty will explain why he worked for such a bad man—so different from him.

"I told Mama what I thought of Yves. I begged her to leave him, but she was terrified of his erratic behavior. I think a part of her was also dependent on him."

"Maybe she was more frightened than dependent. I urge you learn from your Mama's mistakes."

"I have an obligation to Monty. He saved my life. Mama would have wanted it that way."

Cory nodded. "It's proper to show appreciation, but you need expert legal advice to do it the correct way."

"I don't understand," Ashley said.

"You're probably the sole beneficiary of your mother's estate and your obligation to Monty is not only morally correct, but also may be legally appropriate.

You see, his accident occurred during his employment with her. Your mother probably provided insurance for her employees. Are you aware of this?"

"No, no. I'm not." Ashley broke out in a look of dismay.

"Do you know where your mother stored important papers?"

"Mama never discussed business with me. I wish she had. I should have asked her. She was youthful and healthy. We never anticipated her death. In retrospect, I'm at fault; I should have insisted."

"How could you possibly know any better? Unfortunately, most people don't consider these things until they're old—or when confronted with an illness or death of their contemporaries. It is then that their own life expectancy comes to mind and they make wills and execute estate planning," Cory said.

Ashley sighed. "I'm ashamed of my ignorance when it comes to finances. I know how to spend, but I haven't learned how to save. I've never needed to learn."

"A competent attorney will know how to handle your mother's estate and should be able to direct you."

"How can I find one?"

"Phone the San Diego County Bar Association for a referral to an estate specialist. Explain your situation. You'll be provided with a few names of attorneys in the area. Prepare a few questions."

"I'm so ill-equipped." Ashley started to cry.

"You're naturally smart. What you don't know, you can learn. Can you recall going to a bank with your mother?"

Ashley brushed away her tears and nodded. "I just had a flash! I do remember going to a bank with Mama. She introduced me to the manager when we opened an account and also a safe deposit box."

"Was it in this area?" Cory asked

Ashley paused to reflect. "I think so. Oh, yes. I remember walking from the cottage. Yves had left on a business trip for a few days. It was the happiest time we had living here. Janusz and Monty had the time off and were gone a lot. So it was just Mama and I.

"After everyone left, Mama collected most of her jewelry and legal papers and stuffed all of it into a small carry-on sack. I remember strolling arm and arm with her to the bank."

"This may be a good time to walk along that path to help you recall which bank it was. You probably signed something that gives you access to the box."

"Yes. I believe I did, but I don't know where I put the key. Mama told me to hide it to keep it safe."

"We're getting somewhere, Ashley. It's time for you to safely return to the house and look around. There is no one there to hurt you."

"I have the house key, but I don't remember seeing another key. How will I get into the safe deposit box without a key?"

"Let's see. Try to trace your steps from the house to the bank. It's likely on Camino del Mar, the main street with shops and restaurants.

"If you have a problem, another hypnosis session may reveal the location of the safe deposit box key and the bank."

"I'm determined to find that key."

"Okay, but if you don't find it and you locate the bank, ask for the manager. Show your identification—your license and credit card. Explain your situation. If you need to show other information regarding your mother, ask the manager to call the detectives to verify your statement. You probably have their information, don't you?"

"Yes, yes. I have their cards," Ashley said.

"Good. Ask the manager to open your safe deposit box. I don't expect you to have any trouble doing this, but if you do, ask her to phone me. I can vouch that you are a recovered amnesia victim." Cory handed her one of her cards. "In case she wants to confirm."

"Oh, I have so much to do, but this is very important and exciting. I'll call later and let you know what happened. Is that okay, Cory? I hate to impose."

"It is not an imposition. I'm eager to hear from you," Cory replied.

⸗38⸗

With the return of Ashley's memory and Rita's reappearance, Cory felt a great sense of relief. She expected that Ashley would require her services for a while, and that would be manageable.

But, until Ben returned safely to her, she couldn't fully rejoice.

Later that day, Ashley called. "Good news to report. I was about to follow your instructions to the letter, when I suddenly remembered where I had stashed the key. Luckily, it was inside a tiny zippered pocket in the lining of my jacket."

"That is truly wonderful, Ashley."

"I know. It's amazing. Not only that, but just as you suggested, I retraced my steps and easily found the bank.

Once inside, I instantly recognized the woman who had opened our account. She remembered Mama and me. I explained what happened to my mother. She was visibly upset. Her eyes were moist, having recently lost her mother too. We shed some tears together, before we took care of business.

"She had a key that matched mine, and we inserted our keys and unlocked the box together. Then she directed me to a tiny closet with a bench and a shelf and closed the door so I could privately rummage through a ton of mysterious papers. Unfortunately, I could not understand any of them.

"I told her I was very frustrated with the task because I'm unsophisticated in money matters. She recommended a man who works at the bank as an investment advisor to help me decipher the papers and offer his investment advice.

"Mama had once told me not to trust anyone offering big money deals, and to make sure everyone working for me was trustworthy. I wish she had listened to her own advice when it came to Yves.

"I made up my mind not to act impulsively. I'll make an appointment with the advisor and learn a few things from him. But before I make any big investment, I will enroll in a few courses in economics and financial planning at the university."

"Excellent plan. I applaud you, Ashley."

"I trust you, Cory, and I realize I must continue therapy for as long as necessary—until you tell me, I'm ready to stop."

"We'll decide on that together. It's my pleasure to work with you, Ashley."

"Thanks, Cory. How about tomorrow at ten or eleven?"

"Ten tomorrow. I look forward to it."

Cory closed her eyes for a little while, smiling, recalling Ashley's first session. "You've come a long way, baby," she whispered.

⹋39⹋

Her antique grandfather clock had chimed seven times. In between the last two chimes, Cory heard the phone ring and ran to get it, but when she reached for the phone, it had stopped ringing.

Drat! No one had left a message. Hopefully, it was only one of those annoying recorded sales calls that invariably came during dinner despite her entering her phone numbers on the government "Do Not Call List."

Fifteen minutes later, her mouth filled with a bite off the wrap she had prepared of grilled eggplant, red pepper and goat cheese, the phone rang again. She let it ring while she chewed, then picked it up.

"Good ebnin," she said, her mouth still full.

"And good evening to you, lovely one," Ben said.

"Ben?" She swallowed. "Oh, I'm so glad it's you. I've missed you so much. Where are you?"

"I'm at Dulles International Airport. Had to stop off for business for what I expect will take only a day or so, and then I'm on my way home to my sweetie."

She figured he had to be debriefed at one or more of the federal agencies.

"Is there a phone number where I can reach you, Ben?"

"Not yet. I'll call you when I have a new phone sometime tomorrow. I expect to be tied up much of the day, but I'll call as soon as I'm free. Don't worry. All is well. How's my sweetie?"

"Now, that you're almost home, I'm fine. I was worried about you and..."

"Hush. Let's not talk about it now. Save it for later. I love you and will try to make up for my absence—you may see more of me than you expect."

"Do you mean you've put on weight?" Cory snickered.

Ben laughed. "No. It's just that I'm looking forward to hanging out at home a lot. I'm in the mood for some of your healthy cooking."

"Suits me. I've missed you so much, I'm afraid I'll glue myself to you, and you won't be able to go anywhere without me—at least for a few hours!"

"Stop! I'm in a public place," Ben said.

"I love you, Ben," she whispered.

"And I, you. *Ciao*, sweetheart."

Ecstatic in anticipation of having Ben home again, Cory smiled. After his call, her sandwich tasted better. She downed it with water. The water tasted better, too.

An hour later, she turned on the radio to Jazz 88, danced to the Latin rhythm of Cal Tjader on vibes with Stan Getz on sax, and worked herself into a slick, but happy sweat.

She showered, pulled on her pajamas, climbed into bed, closed her eyes, and imagined snuggling with her dear Ben.

In the morning, she awoke fully rested. She grabbed a note pad and wrote a list of Ben's favorite foods, pleased that he looked forward to home-cooked meals and quiet, intimate time to share whatever he could of his experiences abroad. She didn't expect him to tell her everything.

A part-time life with Ben, knowing he was often in danger, was not what she wanted, but she had accepted him "as is", knowing that he thrived on dangerous assignments. It was a price she had initially agreed to pay for the excitement and thrills of being with such a loving, dynamic man. But as time passed, thrills had assumed a more negative position, and danger had become a most unwelcome companion. She considered it a sign of her maturity, but she had arrived at that stage of life ahead of her mate. She figured he would never tire of the excitement. He was drawn to it, like a moth to fire.

Although it seemed apparent that Ben would not change his modus operandi, she couldn't stop hoping he would soon conclude that he had enough dangerous assignments and would eventually ready himself to embrace safer work. Ben had earned a law degree. Perhaps he could find a way to use it to his satisfaction. Teaching or practicing, or writing about the law.

She wondered if he could turn some of his past exciting, dramatic experiences into writing a fictional novel or a play. When the time seemed right, she would suggest this as a potential new vocation, but she wouldn't push it.

If he didn't want to change his work, she could consider a separation. They would no longer live together, but could they remain friends and part-time lovers?

She laughed, realizing that situation was already in place.

Back to square one. She loved him and would accept him "as is."

≠40≠

Two months later, well after Monty's release from the hospital, Ashley felt ready to stop therapy, but she wanted to leave the door open.

"There's a couple of problems left to tackle, but I think I can handle it on my own. I love sharing my life with Monty, but he's not completely comfortable with my taking care of him. I told him it makes me feel good to do things for him and I'm thankful that I can provide enough for us to thrive. But we argue about how much money he costs me, even though I tell him repeatedly that I can afford it and a good chunk was paid by the accident insurance. He also knows I value his companionship. He learns quickly and has become quite the intellectual. We read a lot and discuss books and art. He's my dearest friend."

"That is wonderful," Cory said.

"But here's what I'm worried about. His mother had planned to visit us when he came out of the hospital, but she slipped and fell and was hospitalized for a time. She'll be here next month. I have a lot of apprehension about her visit. I worry that she may not approve of me?"

"Why wouldn't she?"

Ashley's brow wrinkled. "Our backgrounds are so different. She may think, I'm with him out of guilt, and I'll break his heart and leave him when someone in my class and station comes my way."

"I suppose long ago, Brits were more class-conscious," Cory said. "But times have changed, Ashley."

"I'm not so sure of that. Monty hinted that Mum is old-fashioned."

"It's natural to feel apprehension over the situation, Ashley. Monty's mother is probably very appreciative of all you've done for her son. She's raised a good person.

"He wants to be fair to you. He's also smart. You can help him to understand that you don't want him to be dependent upon you forever, just until he's strong enough to manage on his own. Is he interested in learning a new skill that could eventually enable him to find a satisfactory job?"

"We haven't discussed that, but I'll certainly bring it up. I want to be able to turn to you in the future should the need arise, but I don't want to be dependent upon you."

"I know you're completely capable of leading your life well without therapy, but if you get into a bind, I'm here for you. I'm impressed with your progress. You've learned so much about how to manage your finances.

"I'm pleased Ann referred you to me. Oh, by the way, Ashley, where did you meet Ann?"

"I never met her. Just as I told you, I found your card with Ann's name on the back in my purse, but I've no idea how it got there."

"Really?" Cory said.

"Perhaps your card was used as a marker in a library book and I kept it. Whatever. I'm glad I did. You are incredible!"

"I've done nothing extraordinary. I'm your therapist."

Yes, I'm her therapist, Cory thought. It isn't my job to tell Ashley what to do. I should lead, not push or pull. I gave her a compass. Helping Monty would be appropriate and just. It would be Ashley's *mitzvah*.

Epilogue

The Blackmailer was apprehended shortly after her tenth attempt. Her motive was pure greed. A woman in her sixties, she had lost her long-time job as a bookkeeper in a private mental health facility, now defunct. The principals had committed insurance fraud.

Cory overheard Ben talking on his cell phone, "No thanks. I'm no longer interested in that type assignment. I'm considering a career change."

About the Author

Sandra L. Ceren, Ph.D. a native New Yorker resides on the California coast. A clinical psychologist for over forty years she is a Diplomate from the American Board of Family Psychology, and Fellow of the Academy of Family Psychology.

She has appeared on *Oprah*, *Good Morning America* and BBC and has reported on mental health research and answered queries in a weekly health column "Ask Dr. Ceren". This popular column was published in newspapers over many years.

A premarital counseling specialist, her books *Essentials Of Premarital Counseling*, addressed to mental health professionals, and *Look Before You Leap: A Premarital Guide For Couples* were published by Loving Healing Press.

Ceren has a passion for writing fiction. *Prescription For Terror*, the first in her series of psychological thrillers featuring a spunky psychologist/sleuth was published in 1999.

Over a dozen of her short mystery stories have been published in anthologies and magazines including: *Mystery Magazine*, *Detective Mystery Stories*, and *Criminal Kabbalah*.

Also available from Modern History Press